MW01609208

Snow Clues

A Dan Kiraly Mystery

Terez Peipins

ALL RIGHTS RESERVED

No part of this book may be reproduced or transmitted in
any form or by any means, electronic or mechanical,
including photocopying, recording, or by any information
storage and retrieval system, without permission in writing
from the author, except in the case of brief quotations
embodied in reviews.

Publisher's Note:

This is a work of fiction. All names, characters, places, and
events are the work of the author's imagination.

Any resemblance to real persons, places, or events is
coincidental.

Solstice Publishing - http://www.solsticeempire.com/

Copyright 2022 – Terez Peipins

To my father, Jazeps Peipins.

November 15 Amherst, New York

Linda Jackson put down the telephone and glanced at the kitchen clock. She could never get off the phone when her mother called. It was ten past four. Petey should have been home by now; the school bus dropped him off around ten to. As soon as she hung up, Linda rushed to the living room to look out the picture window.

It was already turning into a snowy winter. The school bus left Petey at the bottom of the driveway so he had a hike up to the house on a hilltop. Linda's husband complained that he had to shovel and salt, but the driveway got icy and Petey was terrified of falling down in front of the kids on the bus. Linda couldn't make out any footprints in the snow. Occasionally the driver got delayed so Linda wasn't worried, at least not yet.

Linda put milk on the stove to make cocoa; Petey would be cold and that was his favorite. She put oatmeal cookies on a plate. She drank the remains of her after lunch coffee already turned to sludge. She stood by the window to wait. Petey was so little, small for his seven years. She kept waiting for a growth spurt but it hadn't happened yet. He might take after her; Linda was petite and short.

After ten minutes, Linda put on her coat and boots to see if the bus had come. At the foot of the drive she saw wide tire tracks that could have been from the bus and then tracks in the fresh snow. Her heart started beating faster and faster. There were no more footprints to be seen. "Petey!" she called out into the cold.

Chapter One

Dan Kiraly sat at his desk, rummaging through a drawer looking for a pen that actually wrote. He favored Bics but had a bad habit of gnawing on the ends until they cracked and splintered, at which point he shoved them into a drawer. Today there were no fresh pens so he looked for one that wasn't too badly chewed up. The blinds were drawn on the glass door of his office in an attempt to discourage interruptions but even so his office was rarely quiet.

Two months had passed since the missing person report was filed and Dan knew what that meant. The kid's face was plastered all over milk cartons and missing person posters were hanging in every supermarket in town. Yet there was not one single lead. How far could a seven-year-old boy go? To heaven, was what Dan suspected and the more time that went by the more likely the kid was already dead.

It was always the good ones. Dan hadn't figured out why in all his years on the job. This one was a kid people cared about. Petey's teacher said, "He's such a smart boy, but nice too. He shares things. Everybody loves him." Wasn't that always the case? Dan took the pen out of his mouth.

Dan himself had been taking the boy's picture everywhere from the northern suburbs down to Buffalo. He'd been to every shop in the closest malls and to every neighbor in the vicinity. Nothing had been ruled out. In abduction cases the child was often found close to home but this time there was no lead. Dan had talked to every member of the Jackson's extended family, paternal and maternal.

Then he tried going through the mug shots of every child abuser but he drew a blank there too. His next step had been to search the Internet child porn sites and now, there was nowhere left to look.

"Hey Dan." His buddy, Deke, another police officer called out to him. "Come here, check this out."

Dan followed Deke into the meeting room where a television was blaring. Fox News showed Linda Jackson standing in front of a mound of snow next to her house. "Two months and no one is doing anything. That makes it worse for Petey but, and here her voice broke, "I have to trust in God. He's looking out for my son."

"Hope someone is." Deke muttered as he turned off the set.

"She's saying we're not." Dan shook his head. "How many times does that make it?"

"Local news, practically every night since the kid disappeared. CNN got tired of it, now Fox has the God angle. Got to hand it to her. She's persistent."

"Deke, you know what? You are a cynic."

***

There was an old file from his predecessor, Ted Stevens. Stevens had long since moved on but Dan had kept the old files stuffed in the very back of the grey metal cabinet behind his desk. Maybe Stevens would come knocking on his door to ask for them back but it just meant more clutter. Dan's wife had always accused him of being a pack rat and his office where every surface was covered with folders and files only verified it. Dan was afraid to throw anything out. Who knew when something might come in handy.

There was a list of consultants in the front of the files and Dan racked his brain to try to remember a name. There had been a heavyset woman, bordering on obese who came in leaning on a cane. Stevens had called her in on a case. It was something they kept hush hush and in the more than twenty years Dan had been a cop, it was the only time he'd even seen or heard of anyone calling on a psychic. Now they were television stars; Dan didn't believe in their abilities, but at this point there was nothing to lose. The case was shelved; there were too many missing children. He couldn't let the Jackson case go. He felt sorry for the mother fighting to keep her son's disappearance in the public eye.

The little boy was getting to him. A child lost on his way from the school bus to the front door. Dan rubbed his eyes. He was getting old; he'd seen plenty worse. What had happened? None of the possibilities were pretty. That was what bothered him the most, a very young kid undeserving of such a fate. There were three consultants on the list; he hesitated for a moment before he picked the first.

Jessica Williams. She didn't sound surprised when he identified himself on the phone. She agreed to come to the police station after work.

***

W illiams was certainly not the woman he remembered. He took her dark wool coat, damp from the snow and offered her the chair across from his desk. She shook out her long black hair out, slightly wet from the snow. Dan inhaled a mixture of wet wool and a rich dark perfume, an exotic scent which matched her appearance. He recognized Patchouli; the smell reminded him of head shops an eternity ago.

"I don't have much time. Tax season is coming up so ..." She didn't finish.

"Yes?"

"I'm an accountant."

Her fitted dark suit had him eyeing the frayed cuffs on his shirt sleeves for just a moment. Dan had stopped caring about such things ages ago. He wondered if she even noticed him. Some people, mostly his sister these days, said he was handsome. At 47, he was still in good shape though it required far too many hours at the gym to keep his belly under his belt. He had a full head of brown hair, with just a bit of grey and a nice smile, though these days he wasn't smiling much. He looked kind, his features were soft enough, no sharp edges. " I didn't know."

"Numbers were the farthest I could get from this."

"I told you about the situation on the phone."

"And you're desperate."

"Well."

"I wouldn't be here otherwise."

" Are you comfortable? Tell me what you need." He looked around at his office, the colorless walls that needed repainting, the noise of phones and loud voices just outside the door.

"A little quiet." She looked around the room for a moment. "Do you have a picture or something belonging to the child?"

"I can close all the blinds. That should help." A beautiful woman was in his office; he could imagine the station gossip. Dan reached into his drawer pulling out a plastic bag. Inside was a green stuffed dinosaur that Petey slept with. They'd tried it with dogs to see if they could catch his scent but no such luck. There was his game boy too, found in the snow near the driveway. That was the total of all the evidence there was. Dan handed over the school picture taken that fall, a blond kid with two missing front teeth.

"Could I have some water, please?"

Dan went out to the cooler, glad to have a minute to get his thoughts together. "Weird, this is too weird. I have to be out of my mind." At least she looked perfectly normal. He brought back a Dixie cup of cold water.

Jessica's eyes were closed so Dan could observe her undetected. She had full lips, high cheekbones; hers wasn't a typical beauty. Her milky skin contrasted with her dark hair. His eyes moved down to her legs tucked under the chair. Proper was a word he could use to describe her; everything was in place, make up, no chipped nail polish after a day at work.

When he saw tears running down her cheeks, Dan jumped out of his chair, "Ma'am, are you all right?"

"I saw a place like one of those new housing developments; it's like it's in the countryside but it's not really. In between country and suburb. It looks like a riverbed at the bottom." Jessica stood up. "Just a flash. I saw an old man; he reminds me of Santa Claus. This isn't rocket science. It could just be wishful thinking." She paused to take a deep breath.

If it was a man who looked like Santa Claus it might explain why Petey would get into a stranger's car. *Wishful thinking,* Dan repeated to himself. "Are you sure you're okay?"

"I just have to wash my hands. It disconnects me." She got up and placed Petey's possessions on the desk.

"Can I ask you a personal question? Totally off topic, but I was wondering what your ethnic background was."

"Mongrel American. I think Scottish and some Indian from way back and Russian from my grandmother." She wasn't surprised by the question at all.

"I appreciate your coming in. Thank you."

She shrugged, "That's how it works. I can't give you a street name. I wish I could."

Dan led her to the ladies room and then waited to escort her out. She didn't say what made her cry but it would only confirm what he already suspected.

***

The last few winters had been mild, but this one was setting records for cold and snowfall. Snow had begun in November and hadn't let up since and it was the middle of January. Temperatures were inching up a few degrees so they might get a thaw soon. Dirty snow collected in huge hard mounds, winter in a word, with more shoveling to do before the neighbors complained. The darkness when Dan got home only reflected his mood.

His house was freezing. A timer was set to turn on the heat but hadn't kicked in yet. Without taking off his jacket, Dan turned up the thermostat. The bills would be high, but what could he do? His first apartment had always been at this temperature, barely hovering above freezing. Dan smiled as he remembered it but tonight he realized with a jolt he hadn't come all that far.

Shabby, was how he described his house when he wasn't too busy to notice or care. He and Miranda had bought this big fixer upper to fill with kids but that never happened.

He hadn't been attracted to a woman in ages; Jessica flashed before his eyes. She was different from the women he usually met, younger but with more self-assurance, at least on the surface. It had been a pleasure to watch her without her knowing, intimate in fact; the closest he'd been to a woman in some time.

He sat back in his old recliner and closed his eyes. A place came to him, a construction site about five miles from the Jackson kid's school. It had been in the papers in the fall when a surveyor found flint flakes from an old Indian quarry. The whole project for condos had been temporarily shelved and archeologists had been digging out there until the first winter snowfall. Dan liked the story, the idea that there was more to life than condos; that history counted for something and could even hold up big money on a project like that one.

The next morning he set out with Deke. They'd checked the area already, but a warm spell of 40 degree temperatures meant some of the snow might have melted off.

Deke sank into the driver seat, "A nice little road trip, huh? Haven't we been here before?" He put his coffee mug down and started to unwrap a corn muffin.

"Can't hurt to look again." They rode silently. Dan asked so many questions on the job that here in the car it was a relief not to talk at all. Deke managed to drive and eat at the same time. Dan envied him; Deke was skinny no matter how much he put in his stomach.

When Dan stepped out of the car onto a sheet of ice and almost went down, Deke smiled but didn't dare laugh. "Damn, these boots." Dan cursed.

At the edge of the site there was a small grove of trees the developers left behind so they could call the place Everwood. Deer tracks led down the hill to a ravine. In the old days Dan had done some hunting. He remembered the kick of the rifle and the bullet hitting the flank of his last buck. He fired three times to fell the animal. That was so long ago.

Miranda was furious when he brought the deer home, the stiff corpse tied to the roof of his car."Dan, how could you kill that beautiful animal? What the hell are you going to do with it?" Miranda shouted and then burst into tears. So Dan had turned his car around and took the deer to Deke's. Deke made the arrangements with a butcher to prepare the meat but Miranda wouldn't touch it.

He'd been a fool to listen to a psychic. Here he was, his feet frozen, making his way down to a creek in the middle of January. The creek wasn't completely frozen; water still flowed at some junctures. The ravine was typical of the terrain of the area that had been full of glaciers once upon a time. This was the Tonawanda, a long creek that stretched through a couple of counties in Western New York. In other parts of the country it would be considered a full-fledged river. Dan slid further downhill on the hard packed snow which was nothing like the soft layers of a first snow. His boots were not meant for snowy hikes.

Down on the bank of the creek there was the outline of an object buried in the snow. Dan poked at it. Red appeared. A scarf. It matched the description of what the Jackson boy was wearing. Deke hadn't bothered to venture down to the creek and now Dan shouted so he could hear. "Deke, we got something."

"Coming."

Dan pulled out his cell phone and called the forensic team. "Better get down here." He took photos and marked off the site while Deke stood guard although at this point it was unlikely anyone would disturb the site. A body was face down under a thick layer of snow.

"Maybe the kid froze; that's not a bad way to go." Deke had his own children.

With the time that had passed and the snow that had fallen, there weren't going to be footprints but Dan walked the area, testing the ice to see if he could cross the creek to the other side. He thought better of it. "We need to do something about this snow if we want to see something."

The team arrived in the thirty minutes it took to get there from the station and they set about checking the body. Nothing on the face, but the neck was black. Dan looked away.

"Choked, looks like." Deke said.

"We'll see what the autopsy says." Dan had learned not to make any assumptions no matter how obvious things looked.

By the time they were finished, Dan was cold through and through. He wanted nothing more than to go home and get out of his wet boots but there was the Jackson family to notify.

***

Linda Jackson rushed to the door. When she saw the expression on Dan's face, she gasped. "We're sorry ma'am.

We found your son's body near the creek at the construction site on Watkin's Road.

She put her head in her hands. Dan and Deke waited with her until her husband got home from work. He was angry. "Why the hell did it take so long to find him? He froze out there."

***

"It never gets any easier, does it? " Deke commented as they drove back to the station.

Dan prepared the press release. As far as the parents went, he'd question them in detail again. More than one case had been lost out of sympathy for the bereaved. He couldn't afford to be soft.

By the time he filed the report it was after 7 and he couldn't face going back to his cold house. He punched his sister Maggie's number on his cell. "Have you had supper yet?"

"Come, but bring food. I just got home and I'm beat."

Dan stopped at Wegman's supermarket. He walked through the aisles too distracted to think about food but managed to pick up a roast chicken and a couple of salads. He ended up in the organic junk food aisle wondering if organic could possibly make a difference and eventually opted for a bag of chips.

Maggie always meant peace. Her sons were grown now; Sean was studying biology at Cornell and Todd was trying to figure out what to do with his life. Her divorce was a fading memory and Dan was the closest to a father figure that the boys, now young adults had had.

Maggie was still in her scrubs when she came to the door. She was a surgical nurse who would have made a good doctor if she'd grown up in different times. He hugged her tight. "Hard day?" He spotted bloodstains on her clothes and looked away immediately. It always came as a shock to see something suggesting violence on his sister. He had the monopoly on that.

"A big accident. Stupid kid on a bike slid into a truck. In the goddam snow. We couldn't do anything. Hey, come in. Get warmed up. I'll be right down; I need to shower; I just wanted to get home. There's some wine on the counter."

"Take your time. Take a bath."

"Well, thank you, sir. Maybe I will." She eyed him as only an older sister would. You're hair's getting a bit long. But it doesn't look bad, you look less like a cop." When Dan didn't comment she added. "Are you ok?"

"We found the missing boy."

"Oh." Maggie looked at his face. " Dead?"

"I expected that."

"I'm sorry." Maggie patted his shoulder.

Dan laid the meal out on the table and poured himself a glass of wine. He didn't expect the story to run until the late edition of the news but Cheryl, the chief of police, appeared onscreen in a breaking news report answering questions. Once Dan would have been jealous of someone else breaking the news on TV but that ended just about the time when he felt his job became a burden. Every day brought death, inexplicable pointless death or violent death which was even worse. That's when he lost the ambition that had taken him to detective work and left him stranded there. Even Cheryl had said, "But Dan, you've got a great future. Run for sheriff. Come on. You've got what it takes."

Dan rubbed his eyes and tried not to see the kid's body in the snow bank. To distract himself, he opened the bag of organic potato chips.

"You didn't!" Maggie protested as she came down. "I'm on a diet."

"When have you not been on a diet?" Maggie was about twenty pounds overweight and had been since Todd was born. She was lovely, strong, almost as tall as Dan's 5'10. She smelled of lemons and coconut as she reached past him for a handful of chips.

"That was fast."

"I'm hungry. So tell me what happened."

"Not much to tell. Cheryl was just on the news. I thought it wouldn't be on until 11. I just wrote up the report. Did you invite Todd?"

Maggie shook her head. "No time. You probably see him more than I do." Todd, her son, was living in an apartment in an apartment house that Dan owned.

"Not this week. The last snow was when I saw him. I helped dig him out. When was that?"

"Tuesday, I guess. I'll call him tonight."

"I can stop by and see him."

"No, I don't want him to think we're always checking up on him. How did you find the boy? You were looking for so long."

Dan had been wanting to tell someone who wouldn't laugh. "You won't believe it. I called a psychic."

"You actually believe in that. You're kidding me."

"No, but I found a file with some names and I thought why the hell not, there was nothing to lose. She described a place that reminded me of an article I read. There was a condo development stopped by archaeologists. I went there today with Deke and lo and behold."

"Did you really expect to find the boy there?"

Dan felt a shiver run down his body. "No, well, maybe. I can't say." Dan described sliding down the hill to the creek but left out all the details of the boy. Maggie didn't need to know.

"He was just a baby. Seven years old." Maggie shook her head."So tell me about the psychic."

"She looks normal; she's an accountant and really pretty."

"Ask her out. "

"What if she knows everything about me?"

"Like the guy in the movie whose dick talked. You're afraid she'd guess all your secret motives."

"Not exactly."

"I can't believe it, Dan. You actually believe in that crap."

"No, I'm telling you it was just a freak bit of luck."

"Next you'll be going to Lily Dale to consult with the spirit world."

He'd heard of it but couldn't quite place it. "Lily Dale? Sounds familiar."

"The spiritualist colony on the lake. They've been there since the 1860's or so."

"Are they legit?"

"Who knows for sure? I've never believed that stuff but a nurse at the hospital goes down there for readings. So, ask this woman out."

"What?"

"When's the last time you had a date?"

"Fraternizing."

"You said she didn't take any pay."

"Where's Winnie? I knew there's something wrong when I don't have her begging for food. " Maggie's annoying Airedale was missing and he wanted to get off the subject of dates.

"At the vet's. I dropped her off. Don't ask me how but that dog has a cyst on her butt."

"Is she all right?"

"They're taking it off, then they send it to the lab to analyze it. She's nine, what's that in human years. 63? I think I miss her when she's not here more than I miss the boys."

Chapter Two

Curiosity got the better of him and Dan checked out the Lily Dale website. Lily Dale was a spiritualist colony established in 1879 and was the largest of its kind in the world. He decided to take the afternoon and drive down to the town on Cassadaga Lake, about an hour south of Buffalo. He only had a couple of cases to write up and the autopsy on the boy wasn't finished yet. He could slip away unnoticed before the results came in.

The drive in the summer would be pretty following the vineyards south of the city along Lake Erie. He'd never spent much time down this way but he took advantage to fill his gas tank at the Seneca Indian reservation. The Seneca were able to make a profit on gas and cigarettes, not to mention on the casinos that had sprung up all around the area. Finally, they were able to make some money on what had always been their land. He'd quit smoking about the same time as he stopped drinking or he'd have stocked up on cigarettes too.

"Which way to Lily Dale?"

The station attendant looked at him, "Any trouble down there?"

Dan shook his head; did people immediately peg him as a cop or maybe he just wasn't the typical visitor.

"Not much action there in the winter. But you should see it in the summer, the crowds that go down there."

"Ever been?"

"Me? Hell, no. We got our own thing going. No need of their spirits. But they do readings down there. Is that what you going for?"

"Just some research." That was Dan's stock answer for just about any question he faced. "Looking for some answers."

"Ain't everybody?"

Dan almost turned his car around after he'd been driving about an hour but he finally saw the outline of the lake. He parked in a lot and walked around the small town, streets lined with Victorian houses; most looked closed down for the season though he saw a small fire station and a post office. It was cute in a resort kind of way, but isolated. He couldn't imagine facing a long winter here.

He saw a restaurant and since he hadn't had time for lunch he went in. It was an ordinary cafeteria, with a lingering smell of grease in the air. Dan ordered a turkey sandwich on wheat, and a coffee to warm up. He'd been trying to cut down on coffee since it wasn't doing his stomach any good. Most days he popped antacids like candy but he'd recently gotten down to just four cups a day. This was bad coffee, worse even than at the station where bitter was the norm.

A woman at the next table turned to him. "Are you here to see someone?"

"Not exactly."

"My name is Lillian. I've been here for 30 years. It's pretty quiet this time of year but I like that."

Dan introduced himself."Dan Kiraly." He held out his hand."It's a pretty town." He wondered if she was lonely in such a deserted place. She was in her early 60's, dressed in a pink velour pantsuit that made her look older.

"It's prettier in the summer. You should come back then. We have a wonderful community here."

"So I see. I've never seen anything like it."

Lillian waited a moment, "A spiritual community, you mean?"

"It's for real, isn't it?"

"As real as the table you´re sitting at. At least for us."

Dan let that sink in. "So do you see things?"

"Sometimes. You have two women around you. Your wife; she wants to give you a kick in the pants, just get on with it. The other one, she´s happy; she didn't suffer too bad. It wasn´t what you thought."

"Thank you." Dan's mouth dropped open. Obviously no one had told this woman about his life beforehand. Was this pronouncement better than therapy or were the dead simply more gracious than the living? He wanted to believe his mother hadn't been in too much pain from her long bout with cancer, and that Miranda wanted him to get on with his life. Was it just wishful thinking, like Jessica had said? There was no way to tell.

"Everyone has this ability. Most people are too afraid to even let a little of it in. But you know, you´re a cop. Your intuition probably keeps you alive."

"How did you know?"

"We get officers from time to time. There aren't many men your age coming here alone. If they do, they´re a different type altogether."

"New age types."

"Not somebody in a suit on a Thursday afternoon. Usually the cops sneak in the back door. Don´t want to be seen here in public with the likes of us." She smiled,"Not like you."

"You know, a psychic helped me find someone who was missing."

"The little boy? I saw it on television last night."

"Yes."

"A terrible case. And you don´t know what to think, right? You don´t want to believe it."

"Something like that."

"You better move on with your life or your health will suffer. I´m serious."

"Well, I never expected a consultation thrown in."

"Or wanted it, I bet."

"What do I owe you? "

"Good God, nothing. You just made a winter day a little shorter." She got up to leave. "It's been nice talking to you, Dan."

He made good time back up to Buffalo and was in his office by three. The autopsy report still wasn't ready so he got on the phone to Edgar who wasn't happy to be bothered.

"Give us a break. You'll have it in an hour."

Waiting again. Dan picked up the phone and called Jessica.

"You found him."

"I wanted to thank you. You were a big help."

"I'm glad it was of some use."

Dan steeled himself to ask her a question. "This has nothing to do with the case at all or work and I don't want you to feel under any pressure because of my job."

Jessica interrupted, "Is this something they make you go through? Some kind of training to be politically correct?"

"I wanted to ask you out to dinner, or coffee if you'd prefer."

"Sure."

It was easy. Relief poured over him. "What kind of food do you like?"

"I'm not particular as long as it's not Middle Eastern. My daughter is a strict vegetarian and it seems like that's all she ever eats."

"Would Saturday be okay?"

"My daughter's with her father so you'll save me from a night of watching bad TV and eating popcorn."

When Dan hung up, he asked himself, "Now why the hell did I do that? Do I need problems, is that it?" He was managing well enough without the hassles of dating.

The report was on his desk in an hour. Dan poured himself a coffee and went over it. The body was loaded with barbiturates. Death by strangulation. He was a small child, barely 50 pounds so it didn't take too much force. He'd been in the snow for a while, setting the death back to the day he disappeared, November 15th. The body was dumped near the creek. The little boy had been raped. Dan closed his eyes for a moment. A little boy, for God's sake. But there was no sperm, just the tears in the anus. They'd tried to get some DNA but there wasn't much to be found. Either the killer was an expert or winter had taken care of it. So now what did he have to go on?

Deke came in, "Not good."

"Back to the sex crime files. I'll keep at them."

"The parents."

"Jesus Christ. I'll drive out there. You want to come?" Dan could only hope.

"Take Clarisse. She's good at that sort of thing." She was one of the best detectives in the department.

Dan dreaded seeing the mother again. He called Clarisse and asked her for a favor; and they drove out to what he still thought of as the countryside past the suburb of Amherst.

He'd called to let them know he was coming. Linda Jackson let them in. Her husband, Steve was sitting in the living room.

"Like I told you on the phone, we got the results of the report. I'm sorry to have to tell you, your son was strangled." He let that sink in. "We think it happened quickly. There was sexual abuse. He was drugged at the time so it's possible he didn't suffer."

At that Steve jumped out of his chair and shook Dan by the shoulder. "My son was seven years old.

Clarisse put her hand on his arm. "It's a terrible thing."

Linda Jackson face went cold and she crumpled onto the floor. "Petey."

When they left the house, both were silent. Finally Clarisse said. "I never want to do that again. He was just a baby for God's sake."

Dan dropped her off at the parking lot and then drove home. He should start on the files again but he had lost heart. There would be time enough later. He turned up the heat and then went to look for his tool box, first pouring himself a large whiskey. He needed it. Then he went upstairs. He'd been meaning to fix the bathtub drain for ages.

***

Dan looked at himself critically as he got ready for his date. He didn't want to look too formal but after years of wearing a uniform, or dark jackets and pants, he just couldn't do casual. He put on a thick blue sweater, his Christmas gift from Maggie and his only pair of corduroy pants. That was a step up from jeans. He aimed for cool but doubted he was even in the neighborhood.

All those years ago, Miranda picked out his clothes; he never took the time. The rest of him wasn't bad, a bit of grey around the temples, but mercifully, he still had a full head of dark brown hair. He had warm honey colored skin, lines etched into his face by a nice smile. Warm brown eyes. People usually responded positively to him, trusting him instinctively.

The body took work. No matter how many crunches he, there was still a layer of fat around his stomach. Dan wasn't all that tall, so he couldn't afford to look like a block.

Jessica had chosen a Thai restaurant tucked away in a shopping plaza on a highway. Dan was halfway through a tumbler of water wishing it was something stronger when Jessica arrived.

He helped her take off her coat and handed it to the waiter. She unwound a red scarf which matched the flush of her face. She wore a dark green sweater, almost black but it was soft looking, most likely cashmere. Dan wanted to reach across the table and touch it.

"You look very nice." She probably got tons of compliments and he knew he wasn't being original.

"Thank you."

When Jessica ordered a beer, Dan felt relieved. A buzz would help him through the evening. They looked at their menus and decided on coconut soups and curries.

"I'm starving. I didn't have time for lunch."

Dan felt too nervous to feel hunger. He hoped the spicy food wouldn't give him too much grief. One thing he was used to was asking questions so he started in right away. "How long have you had your.." He paused for a moment, trying to think of the right word.

"Gift?" she asked, smiling. "It's the nice way of saying it. All my life. I used to wish I didn't."

"I went to Lily Dale."

"Really? What'd you think? That they're all crazy out there."

"No. I only talked to one person who gave me some advice I didn't ask for."

"I bet."

"What does it feel like? This gift?"

"Sometimes I see faces of people, sometimes I feel something, sadness, cold; a feeling or sensation. Most of the time I don't know the people I see. Sometimes it's only an image I get. Usually none of it lasts very long, like a march of strangers through the brain."

"Does it bother you?"

"It used to, but I've been probed and tested. " She held out her upturned palms. "See, no weird signs on my palms. I'm not crazy. Even the shrinks say so."

"I didn't mean that. I was just wondering how it felt. How did you become an accountant?"

"Well, I don't channel lottery numbers. I like numbers, they are predictable. They are always right."

"Can you tell who's cheating on their taxes?"

"Only by the numbers. Hey, can I interrogate you for a change?"

"I'm sorry. I was just curious."

"I'm teasing. Why are you a cop?"

"A detective. Why do you ask?"

"Questions with questions."

"I'm used to finding answers. Now if I could do it like you do." For a moment he wondered if she could see what the women in Lily Dale claimed to see around him.

They were on to jasmine tea after the plates were cleared. Jessica asked him, "Have you been married?"

"My wife passed away or should I say passed over." He tried to lighten the topic. Years later and it still required an effort to say she was dead.

"I'm sorry. Do you have children?" He shook his head. He didn't say they had been trying for such a long time. She didn't press on.

"My daughter, Christine, is twelve. I've been divorced two years; my ex has custody so he gets the joys of adolescence and I get every other weekend. He thought I was a bad influence on her." Her dark eyes grew sad.

"What'd he think, you were like Samantha in Bewitched, a wrinkle of the nose and you'd make him disappear? " Dan was still trying to be light.

"I wish I could. He was afraid I'd predict something bad, but it doesn't work that way or maybe he was afraid I knew him too well. I never did though. I still can't figure him out."

They split the check. As they stood up to leave Dan asked, "Would you like anything else, a drink, an ice cream?"

"It must be all of ten degrees out there. I don´t think anyone´s suggested ice cream to me since I was Chris's age."

He walked her to her car, a Honda. Safe and reliable he thought; after all, she was a mother. She´d look better in a sports car, like the red Mustang he lusted after when he was a teenager. Dan wanted to put his arms around her, but she held out a gloved hand. He brought it to his lips.

That got a laugh. Dan willed himself not to be pushy. "Thank you. It´s been very nice."

"Informative?"

"I didn´t want to sound like a detective."

"Well, we can´t stand out here all night. It´s freezing. Would you like to have a drink? I don´t have a big selection of drinks but I´m sure I can find something.

He followed her car to a neighborhood with big houses and even bigger yards.

The house wasn´t like Dan´s; there was no need to turn up the heat as soon as they walked in. The walls were wallpapered, striped with the furniture a deep burgundy to match. There were flowered cushions and yellow cushions. It struck Dan as fussy, as if she had taken too many ideas from magazines and tried to put them all together in one room, or someone had done it for her.

He sunk down into the sofa. "No crystal ball?" he teased.

"No gun?" was her answer.

"Sometimes. Not when I´m off duty." He could have said how much he hated carrying one. Carrying made him uncertain of what exactly he was supposed to do with it, or worse, knowing exactly what he needed to do and not feeling up to it.

What was the next step with Jessica? For so many years he had only had sex when he was drunk. Without booze there was a missing step. He worried his body wouldn't respond the way he wanted it to.

"What can I get you? Let's see, wine, and I have brandy and beer."

"Whatever you're having is fine."

Jessica returned with beer. "I didn't want to mix."

"That's fine." She sat down on the edge of the sofa. Dan took her hand so she would slide into the cushions where he was sitting. "Soft sofa."

"My husband picked it. I can't get up from it."

Dan felt electric pinpricks the length of his body where they were touching. He closed his eyes for a moment.

"No falling asleep."

"Impossible. If just touching your hand makes me feel like this."

She kissed him. He felt like a teenager, wanting to tear off her clothes and get to it. It seemed like years since he'd been with someone rather than months. "Do you want to...."? He tried to think of a way to say it.

In answer Jessica pulled her sweater up over her head. Dan caught his breath, "Is it okay here?"

"The bedroom is where my husband..."

He unsnapped her bra, kissing her neck and working his was down to her breasts, small and firm. Her nipples were hard, but it could be the cold.

"You're good at clothes."

"You'll have to help me with the rest." He unzipped her boots and she pulled her jeans down over her hips. Without a question she had a gorgeous body. He paused as he took it in; he didn't want to get too excited too fast.

"You have to take off yours too."

It was never a graceful moment and now here they were on the overstuffed sofa in full light. He hoped she wouldn't notice the rounded belly he couldn't get rid of. And he was 47 about a decade older than she was. She started on his shirt.

He felt he'd had a slight erection since he'd first seen her. At least that part of his body was hard. She had her hand on it. "I'll come too fast." He said to her. He concentrated on her body, kissing each part of it. "Tell me what you like."

"Just keep doing what you're doing. " He had his hand between her legs, building up to a rhythm.

She helped him put a condom on. Afterwards she lay on top of him.

"I should go before I fall asleep." Dan shifted his body. His arm was asleep.

"You can stay." She led him into the bedroom which was clutter free. A quilt covered the bed. Jessica handed him a towel and toothbrush. "I have a supply. Chris always forgets hers.

Dan was fighting off sleep. "You don't have any pictures of her."

"I'm still pissed off at them. They ganged up on me; they thought there was something wrong with me. I'm an accountant for God's sake." Dan pulled her nearer.

He woke in the middle of the night, his stomach on fire from the spicy dinner. He checked her medicine cabinet for antacids but no luck. Finally he found a Tums stuck in the corner of his coat pocket. He sat for a moment in the living room bending over.

Jessica came in. "Are you all right?"

"Yes, it's just my stomach. Acid. It's not an ulcer; if it were it could be cured. Could just be stress."

"And Thai food, all that hot pepper. Do you need anything?"

"I took an antacid. Thanks."

"Are you going to be able to sleep?"

In the morning he woke disoriented. He'd been dreaming of his backyard when he was a kid and Miranda dressed in a flowing white gown floating through the air.

Dan was saying to her, "Come in, it's cold. You'll catch your death." He shivered as he remembered the words.

Jess was in the kitchen, "How are you this morning?" Her tone sounded sharp like one she'd use with her daughter when she was late for school.

"Fine, thanks. Did you sleep well?"

She nodded. Jess was a person who woke decisively, no long slow mornings for her. She was dressed and ready to go. "Coffee?"

"Please."

"Breakfast?"

"Oh, no, thank you."

"Toast or cereal? You're sure?"

"Thank you, really but I should go."

"Don't tell me you do church."

He shook his head. He needed more time to wake up to be able to have a conversation.

"What do you usually do on Sundays? I hate them."

"I read the paper if I'm not working." The first sip of coffee was clearing his head. The problem would be when it hit his stomach. "Then, I check out the rental property I have. My nephew lives in one so I visit with him; sometimes we watch TV. Don't laugh."

"Football is almost over. Baseball hasn't started. What do you watch, hockey?"

Anything really. I've been known to watch tennis but I draw the line at golf."

"Thank god for that."

"So you see, it's not that exciting. What do you do?"

"When Chris is here we fight and shop and go out for lunch. If she's not, I see friends; we go to the movies or dinner. But I don't go out that much. My ex was into socializing big time so I'm still recovering. We sometimes had dinners for 20."

"No kidding."

"Craig had all kinds of ambitions. I guess I was a liability."

"How long ago?"

"We were together six years. Then two years apart but the divorce took longer. Stupid state this one. We had to go through mediation. Then custody."

"You must of got married young."

She shrugged, "24."

"You're still young."

"38. Believe me, I don't feel young."

"You look wonderful. Can I call you or if you want, you can call me. I have to get started on that exciting day I've got planned." He kissed her on the mouth.

But instead of heading home, Dan headed for the station and sat with the autopsy report and the photos spread out on his desk. He tried to keep his eyes from focusing too long on the images. It was a slow Sunday which meant Saturday night had been quiet. There were two messages from Linda Jackson asking about any progress they had made.

The snow had kept the body fresh as a rosebud according to Cheryl. He wondered just how many sins the snow could hide. The rape still shocked him. What was also surprising were the barbiturates. With a controlled substance they might be able to get a lead but then again it could have come from the street. Deke was on that, checking prescriptions in the drugstores in the area.

Plenty of trace evidence on the clothing if you wanted to call it that. Kids played on rugs, touched each other, rolled around in each other's DNA, so to speak. There were some fibers, a few hairs, and particles. No matches on anything. That just meant they didn't know what the source of any of it was.

Dan tried to imagine the sequence of events. The guy picked up the boy, drugged him and then had his fun? At least that was what Dan hoped. But why kill him unless that was part of the thrill? If the kid had been drugged he wouldn't have caused the guy any grief but he was so small he couldn't have been hard to handle.

Was the strangling just going one step too far? Now this was where he could use some of Jessica's powers. The crime made no sense. The guy should have been choking himself to get off, not choking the kid. Why drug the kid? Why was there no DNA anywhere? A condom? Too many questions and a big fat zero in the answer department.

Dan's head felt fuzzy; he hadn't really slept well with his stomach in upheaval. He hadn't forgotten Jess had mentioned someone who looked like Santa Claus. After three hours of looking at files of sex offenders he decided to call it a day and head home.

As soon as he got in and was changing his clothes, Todd, who had his own set of keys to the house, called up the stairs. "I called last night but you weren't here. A hot date?"

"Something like that."

"All right, way to go." Todd sounded surprised.

"So what's up?"

"Can't get the car started. Probably it's the battery."

Dan liked to feel useful. "Well, let's go take a look at it."

Chapter Three

On Monday, Deke was following up the drug lead and Dan was back at the computer screen. So was it a carefully planned crime with the perp knowing exactly what time the kid got off the bus or was it all a series of chance events? School buses were regular and had been since Dan was a child. 4 pm was an off hour. The murderer could be unemployed or someone working odd hours. A man could easily carry a child's weight; for that matter a woman could too. He went over his notes for the meeting with Cheryl at 10.

There were the four of them; they'd worked together many times before. Deke did the background checks; Clarise did the questioning, and increasingly, Dan did the paperwork, except on this case. Cheryl just busted their chops. "So what have you got?" Today Cheryl was in a pinstripe suit, looking like a female mafia boss. Dan would normally tease her about her fashion choices but today was not the day.

He repeated the information on the Nembutal and the strangling though she had gotten the same report.

So far Deke had nothing and Clarisse was back to the same area, talking to anyone she could find who might have noticed anything out of the ordinary. They'd been through all of this back in November.

"We're looking for the vehicle. How did he get the body down there?" Cheryl threw out the question.

"He's small, so it's not too hard to carry him. It's not even a quarter mile from the road. If he crossed the creek it's even closer."

"Who have we talked to down that way?"

"All the construction guys that pass by to make sure their trailer is still standing. It's deserted now since they can't do any work until the snow melts. There isn't much else; the mall is about five miles down the road. The first round we didn't get that far from the kid's house."

"Can't hurt to ask again if anybody saw anything. Let's see what we can come up with. We can meet tomorrow. Same time. The school teacher wants to see someone. Dan?"

***

Live by the sword, die by the sword was Dan's motto. This applied to him too, but he'd been lucky so far. Only one gunshot wound from a crazy guy holed up in an apartment, shooting at anything that moved. The bullet got his shoulder; he had a scar beneath the shoulder blade. He'd kept the bullet as a souvenir. Then he'd been stabbed in the stomach while breaking up a bar fight. Thank God, he was off the beat. These days he mostly just went in to figure out what happened after the fact.

Dan looked over the report. A. A gang murder again and the police had already picked up a suspect which was lucky. Often no one talked. Dan would go over later and talk to the officers but it could wait. He had more papers with the lab results. Cheryl insisted on endless details; it meant every little thing was documented and their asses were covered.

He said the name to himself, "Petey." He preferred to say "the kid". Visiting the kid's school would most likely not bring any information.

Dan took a deep breath as he entered the classroom. A memory of Miranda came back to him though he rarely visited her first graders after they got married. The kids were young enough to be impressed when he wore his uniform. Later, there never seemed to be enough time for visits and Miranda eventually stopped asking.

Mrs. Dombrowski shook his hand. Dan surveyed the room with its child size chairs, the red hearts on the bulletin board ready for Valentine's Day. The kids lived from one holiday to the next. Miranda had boxes of arts and crafts from papier-mache turkeys to Earth Day posters, one of her favorite holidays. The boxes were still somewhere in the basement. Dan made a mental note to get rid of them.

"It's been very hard for us."

"I can well imagine." Dan took a deep breath.

"He was one of the most popular kids. At that age they don't expect to lose a classmate."

Dan nodded, in this middle-class neighborhood they wouldn't. He waited for her to go on. He got the picture; she didn't have any information. She just wanted to connect with someone who might be able to explain such a horrible death, as if there were any way to do that.

She pulled out a poster the class had made for Petey. There was a picture of him in the center and messages scrawled in kids' hands around it."His classmates made it. I'll give it to his parents."

"I'm sure they'll appreciate it." As Dan looked at it, he choked up.

"I was thinking you could come and talk to my class. You know, to help them feel safe again."

"We have an education department that deals with that. I don't have much experience with kids. I'll give you the person to contact."

***

Ten years ago Dan had exchanged his uniform for a suit and by this time his suits needed replacing. He was excited when he first started as a detective; Miranda was too. She shopped with him and picked out the three dark suits he was still wearing. That was just about when the drinking started getting heavy. It shouldn't have come as a surprise; they'd met in a bar and most of their social life consisted of going out for dinner and drinks. A decade lost was how Dan saw it now and Miranda was his biggest loss of all.

He'd tried everything to exorcise her from his thoughts. In the beginning there were plenty of women; Maggie called them the toos- too pretty, too young, too crazy; there was always something wrong with them. Mostly the problem was that they weren't Miranda, so he just gave up dating. If he wanted to get laid, there were other recourses. It couldn't have been easier and there was one woman he saw about once a month or so, Valerie. He had no idea if that was even her real name. He never told his sister who would have been shocked but it worked. He wasn't sure he was capable of a normal relationship though with what he knew so far of Jessica he suspected with her a relationship wouldn't be casual.

Maggie called as soon as she found out Dan had been on a date. "So, tell me."

"Nothing to tell."

"The psychic? You work fast. Are you going to see her again?"

He didn't answer but let Maggie go on. It ran in the family, all the questioning.

"So, come on, tell me."

"She's a deep person."

"Problematic."

"I didn't say that."

"Oh." Maggie stopped.

"Look, I'm fine. I need to get back to work. Thanks for calling. I'll call after I get somewhere with this case, ok?"

***

When Dan tried to sleep, all he could see, and worse, feel was Jessica, her body, her lips. He got up and took a sleeping pill; he needed to be able to think in the morning.

It was more of the same when he got to the office. Cheryl called him in; her office was in the corner, with no blinds hiding a view of the skyline with the lake in the distance. "Dan, we've got to make some headway."

"We're on it. Believe me. I've got the mother breathing down my neck. There's nothing I want more than to find this guy."

"One like that on the loose. We can't have it."

"Give me another pair of hands."

"You know I can't do that. We're short as it is." There was the ongoing problem of budget cuts.

"We got Clarisse checking the mall for any clues. We went house by house in the area where we found him. I got a list of drugstores that filled scripts for Nembutal. We checked vets in the area. We're working on it."

The size of his cubicle always hit home after a visit to Cheryl's office. Once Dan thought that the supervisor job was his, a given.

Dan's hand was poised over the phone. "Can I ask you for a favor?"

Jessica answered, "You want me to see what I can do."

"I wouldn't ask but we're getting nowhere but don't take it as an obligation. I'd still like to see you again whether or not..." And it was true, his body was calling out for her. His heart was beating faster, just hearing her voice.

"Ok."

"To which?"

"Both."

"Great, I can't tell you how much I appreciate it. Let me know what's a good time."

"I'll check my schedule and get back to you."

***

The phone rang; there was a suicide out at the State University. 19-year-old John Sullivan. Dan took down the information and drove out to the Main Street campus with Deke. The victim lived in a house he shared with other guys on Winspear Street. The neighborhood was a student ghetto, known for wild parties and occasional violence.

The body had been moved already. His room was cordoned off. The campus police were quickly on top of things. They showed Dan the gun. Since the crime took place off campus, Buffalo police were involved.

"Was there a note?"

"We're checking his computer."

In the living room, the roommates were shaken but helpful. Alex said, "I didn't know he had a gun."

Dan felt sorry for them.

"He was quiet." Alex blinked away his tears.

Dan finished questioning him and moved on to the other two boys. He wouldn't want to be in their shoes. Sullivan had shot himself at 10 AM when the rest of them were in class. Alex found him when he got back at 11:30. The campus police arrived half an hour later. The autopsy would show if any drugs were involved but from this vantage point it looked pretty straightforward.

Dan didn't get why he did it on a Monday morning. The boy had gotten through the weekend, which was usually the hardest time for loners. Monday meant back to a routine but it might have been the only time he could be alone in the house. At the very least the boy hadn't taken anyone with him; campuses these days were not the safest places to be. Dan sometimes worried about his nephew out at Cornell.

After Dan bagged the weapon, they were headed out. "What a place." he commented.

"It's not so bad."

Imagine living there with three other guys. What a mess."

"Those kids were ok. Hockey fans."

"Suppose you don't like sports." Dan said and then dropped it.

So far they had a suicide, and two robberies. Robberies were pretty constant and then there were drugs; a mean business, drugs. After that there were the lost souls of the city who most people didn't see. Downtown was filled with street people. There were those so desperate they lined up to sell their blood for twenty bucks. And then headed to the churches for the free meals.

***

Jess called him back, "I can come after work today."

"What time should I expect you?"

"Is 7 too late?"

"Perfect." Dan didn't leave the station earlier than that most days. "I can buy you dinner." It was only Monday so he hadn't held out for very long at all.

Jess was punctual. Today she was wearing a red coat. Heads turned as she walked through the department and into his office.

Dan closed the door behind them and took her coat. "How was your day today?"

"Ok." She shrugged." Shall we get to it?"

Dan closed the blinds and took out the pictures again. He handed Jess the dinosaur he had kept in his drawer along with other scant evidence. For a moment he paused to identify it; years ago films made dinosaurs popular and then almost just as quickly they were forgotten except by little boys. This was one of the big gentle ones, a brontosaurus.

Jess took it in her hands and closed her eyes. Dan watched her again; her long black eyelashes fluttered. He saw dark circles this time and the start of wrinkles around her eyes, crow's feet weren't they? They were supposed to show character. She was about Miranda's age when she had died. He blinked to stop Miranda's face from invading.

Jess opened her eyes, "That old man again. White hair, a beard. A dark car. That's it. I'm sorry."

Dan handed her a cup of water, "Are you all right?" Jess nodded. "Would you still like to have dinner?"

"I'd like a burger." They stayed downtown and went to a bar. It was Monday night so it wasn't crowded. Only the diehards were out on a Monday night; Dan knew because he used to be one of them. He ordered a beer and looked through the menu for something that was not too caloric. He chose a salad and the waitress got their orders mixed up, setting the salad down in front of Jess.

She ate quickly, "I didn't have lunch today."

"Thanks for coming. I know you're busy."

"No leads I take it."

Dan shook his head. "It's been dragging, what with all that time it took to find him. It's a pretty cold trail." Dan concentrated on his salad though the burger looked much better.

"Want some fries?"

"Worse than the burger. It's the oil."

Jess smiled, "Thanks for that. What are you, a health nut?"

"No, I'm trying to lose some weight, that's all. If I were your age, I'd still be eating burgers."

"How old are you?"

"47."

"That's not old. What do they say, 50 is the new 30."

"I'd stay with 30."

"You haven't got a motorcycle yet. Maybe that comes later."

"I've thought about it." Dan laughed. "That's what midlife is all about now; you get on a bike and gun the motor." He paused for a moment, not quite sure how he was going to talk about it. "I had the feeling that you didn't really enjoy the other night." He left it short of saying sexually. So then, I was wondering why not?"

"God, you're direct, aren't you?"

"I had an entire marriage where I didn't talk."

Jessica thought about it for a moment and then she answered the question. "I guess I wanted to feel something different, maybe have more fun. It doesn't seem possible anymore."

"I understand, I think." He smiled at her, "I could try to make it more fun."

"It's me, not you. You remember that Schwarzenegger film set in the future and he goes to a travel agency and they offer him a trip where he can be another person. That's what I want. Just to get away from myself."

***

Dan got on the computer and continued checking sites looking for an old guy with a white beard. "It could be a costume," he thought to himself. "It doesn't have to be literal. This gift of Jessica's was driving him nuts; nothing was what it appeared to be. Here he was back at zero again with just an image to go on.

Pedophiles were present on the net but that sexual inclination usually got a person into trouble somewhere along the way. There were lists to go through; neighborhood associations kept tabs of known sex offenders and tried to stop them from moving in. There were ways a detective could find them.

When Dan did his stint as an altar boy, Father Joe once rested his hand on his leg. Creepy, but it never went further. The hand kneaded his thigh but didn't reach his crotch. Dan never mentioned it; in those days nobody did, but he knew he was lucky that's all that happened. His mother baked pastries and cakes for the priest who was like a God in their neighborhood. This particular one would be long dead. Dan rubbed his eyes. Lawsuits against the church were a dime a dozen now.

***

At three AM, Dan woke, gasping for breath. It was the dream again. Sometimes it happened underwater when he couldn't get up to the surface to breathe. Sometimes he was being chased in an alleyway which led to getting trapped at a dead end. Or worst of all, he was driving, heading straight for the guardrail, like in a bad TV movie. Death dreams, he called them. He always woke the instant before a bullet hit him, or the car hit the rail, or when he went underwater for the last time.

He wondered if the dreams were a premonition, but he'd only had then since he left the beat. It was getting old, that's what it was. Fear was weighing heavily on him and he no longer felt fast and strong enough to escape.

Could Jessica see when he would die? There were plenty of ways to go and he'd experienced them all nightly. But there was no way he could ask her; she'd think he was completely crazy. Besides, she'd done enough. He might just as well start calling those 800 numbers for advice since he was going soft in the brain, actually thinking she could give him answers.

When he got to work, slightly groggy from the restless night of sleep, Linda Jackson was waiting for him. He led her into his office. She looked thinner and paler than just a couple of weeks ago. "Can I get you a cup of coffee?"

She shook her head. "Tell me what you've found."

"I want you to know we've been working hard. There are several leads we're looking into. We're making some headway." He lied and felt bad.

"Tell me."

"I can't give you the details just now." Her phase of anger was over and now she was just broken. "I really am sorry. Let me get you that coffee." He was afraid she'd be crying when he came back. He put down the cup along with a couple of creamers and packets of sugar.

Mrs. Jackson picked up the cup without paying much attention. "You have to find him. You have to do something; I can't bear it."

"We're doing everything we can. I promise you. We'll find him." Dan lied. With all the time lost, he was beginning to doubt they'd ever find the killer.

When he got her out of the office, Dan felt worse. There was nothing to go on. His internet searches came up with zilch. Thousands of pages of shit out there which was disgusting. He'd seen his share of the underside of life but what was done to children was appalling. The kids were the powerless, helpless ones. When he looked at the pages, he felt relieved he hadn't brought a child into the world.

Every neighbor within several miles of the Jackson's house and the construction site had been questioned. One kid said he saw a funny looking car, but there hadn't been anything unusual about any of the vehicles Dan saw in the vicinity. He combed the neighborhood again, checking all the neighbors' vehicles again and found the usual Toyotas and Hondas, with an occasional BMW, nothing special.

There were always people who wanted to feel important or share the limelight, even when it was associated with this hideous crime so Dan investigated all calls or reports with a degree of caution. Deke came in, took one look at Dan and said, "Not going well."

"That's pretty obvious. Such a little boy, raped, let's say ripped open, drugged. What else am I missing?"

"Could have been someone passing through the area. Sees this cute little kid, stops the car, tells him a story."

"He could be in Mexico by now."

Deke shrugged. "Or he could still be right here. We gotta find something."

"Cheryl's already on my ass. The mother came in again."

"Tell Cheryl you need more help. I can't talk to those folks again. With all the other shit happening. Just you and me and Clarisse when they can spare her, come on. " Then Deke smiled and raised his eyebrows, "Hey, I hear you've got a girlfriend."

"Yeah?"

"Come on, you can tell old Deke about it."

"Just a friend."

The conversation made him think of calling her. What were the old rules? He hadn't dated in such a long time he barely remembered. Was it Wednesday? You couldn't call later than that to make plans for the weekend. Yeah, that was it. He needed something to get his mind off the kid. He called Jess.

"I've got Cris this weekend. We could go out tonight."

Going out weekdays or any day hadn't been part of his life for years. Dan checked his shirt hoping it didn't smell of sweat and it wasn't too wrinkled. There wasn't time to go home and change since they were meeting downtown again. They ate at a Vietnamese restaurant, big soups that were warming and soothing. When they finished, Jessica asked, "Do you want to have a drink or is it too late?"

It wasn't even nine. "Sure. It's not late unless you're a toddler.'

"How about your house?"

He tried to remember if Martha, the woman who cleaned once a week, had come by. Miranda had hired her, and all these years later, Dan kept her on even though he didn't make much of a mess or even spend much time at home. As soon as he got in, Dan lit a fire so the place would look cozy if that were possible and then brought her a rum on ice.

"It's delicious; it tastes like caramel."

"It's from Haiti."

They sat on the old and shapeless sofa in front of the fireplace. Dan hoped she wasn't paying attention to the decor. "I can try to make it fun." He massaged her feet which made her laugh. "See, you can laugh."

They ended up in bed. Dan liked to think it proceeded better than the previous time but he wasn't completely sure.

Jessica asked him, "Your wife died a long time ago. Have you had any relationships since?"

"Not really. Hard to follow Miranda. I wasn't ready for a relationship. I went out but nothing serious."

"What do you do, well, for sex?"

"I have a friend, a woman I know."

"What do you mean, a woman you know?"

"I'm not sure what term to use."

"A prostitute? An escort?"

"I guess that would do."

"Like a politician. Why would you do that?"

"It's easy."

"It's so macho."

"That's me. In a nutshell."

"When you were married, too?" She didn't drop it.

"No, of course not. Afterwards, when I didn't want any complications."

"I don't get it.'

"It's a transaction that makes it simple. It's not like I did it regularly." Dan didn't say"do"; he didn't want Jessica to think badly of him.

"You mean sex with no emotional investment. It's safe?"

"Of course."

"Do you know that having sex with a person creates karma?"

"What the hell does that mean?" Dan was left to ponder the thought.

In the morning Dan asked her, "Can you wear the same clothes to work today?"

"I'm doing an audit today in a different office."

"Do they know about your other life?"

"I don't tell them. It never comes up."

Dan lathered her hair and rinsed it in the sink. They ended up back in bed and he finally felt her come, pushing him over the edge.

"I need a hair dryer."

Dan produced one for her, back from the days he actually styled his hair. He'd be late for work but it was worth it.

***

"You haven't asked me to do your taxes yet." Jess commented later on the phone.

"My cousin does them. Besides you don't want to know what I earn. I'm a public servant."

"I have Chris again."

"Oh." Dan really didn't know what to say. Jess called just to talk.

"The first day is hard and then when it's okay she has to go."

"That is hard. Can't she live with you?"

"If she changes her mind but she's stubborn. She refuses to say it was a mistake. Craig is much stricter; he doesn't have a clue about what a girl needs. He's an asshole." She paused for a minute. "Sorry. I just get started and I can't stop."

"It's ok."

"Next weekend then."

"No problem." Dan was a bit relieved. He needed some time since he wasn't sure what he wanted. Maybe it was already too late. Maggie would challenge him, what were you thinking. He'd be the asshole in this. Things were getting better with Jess, at least sexually after the first time but it was probably never going to be wildly passionate. When he first met Miranda he couldn't believe the places they managed to do it, wedged into corners and backseats. The years had taken their toll, his body felt denser, slower to react. Maybe that was the difference.

Chapter Four

After another day with no leads, Dan took tilapia out of the freezer when he got home. He'd have dinner late but it didn't matter. What was that fish really, where did it come from? What did it look like?" He'd fished Lake Erie with his dad but they threw back everything they caught off the break wall. There was too much mercury in the lake fish even back then. But back then fish were simpler, trout and sunfish that sparkled out of the water. There was nothing with strange names that came from a farm.

Memories assaulted him from all directions. Was that what going out with Jess meant? Remembering?

In the bottom drawer of his desk was a box of photos, a mix of everything that dated all the way from his mother up to Miranda. Everyone in those photos was gone now except for him and Maggie. He felt the weight of that when he opened the box.

Who'd have to go through his crap when the time came? Maggie, probably. Dan had accumulated more junk but the house still felt like everything had stopped in 1997. After Miranda died, he replaced the furniture; he couldn't bear her presence everywhere. He'd just gone into a furniture showroom and said,"I need a living room, bedroom, hell, I need stuff for a house." Now, the only thing he actually liked was the big leather armchair that sat in the corner of the living room.

That would be a project to work on, re-doing the rooms. Judging from HGTV, it was what that occupied middle America. Or he could just sell it and get a condo but he liked living in a neighborhood and having neighbors. More than one person commented on how safe they felt with his living right there on the block. These days, African refugees lived across the street wearing bright clothing and carrying babies in their arms. Sometimes he helped them get their cars started in the winter thinking their lives held more hope than his.

This wasn't how his life was supposed to be. He was supposed to be with Miranda, no booze but at least three kids and the possibility that life could be good. Sometimes he could picture it. Miranda was holding a chubby blond baby who looked just like her, and he would be standing behind her, the smiles of satisfaction on their faces, enormous.

Miranda was the star of high school. He hadn't known to what extent until they went to her tenth reunion. Everyone had expected something more from her, not to be a school teacher married to a cop. Maybe they even dreamt of Hollywood or, at the very least, a rich husband. They viewed him with disappointment. On top of the pile was her prom queen photo. Dan dumped it in the trash.

She'd stayed alive in his mind all this time with their imagined relationship improving to the point there were no slamming doors, no screaming matches, no driving off in a rage. There was no garbage can filled with glass bottles. This Miranda of his mind was solicitous, always generous, and unfailingly gorgeous.

Miranda had always worked. She was a functioning alcoholic. Dan had assumed since she got herself off to school every day, everything was okay. Miranda usually started on wine when she got home, sometimes asleep on the sofa before Dan got back from work. In the beginning, Dan joined her but then couldn't keep up. His stomach problems were the legacy of his marriage.

Miranda was a real blond, never fake roots showing through. The pictures shocked him again, her sheer beauty moved him; she'd grown fuzzy in his mind which was how he liked to keep her. He had to force himself to keep rooting through the box.

She had pink lips in a bow shape, alabaster skin, and that long lithe body that revisited him at night. No wonder no one had been able to compete. She was a goddess who looked down upon him from a sacred mountain. Maybe he should just set up an altar to her and be done with it. The external rather than the internal presence could take over; then, maybe he could be free of her.

***

Dan picked up the report of the interviews Deke and Clarisse had already looked at. No leads since the Petey went missing. No neighbor was close enough to hear or see anything. The Jacksons lived in an old farmhouse that the suburbs were closing in on but hadn't quite arrived to. Petey was the second to last kid to be dropped off from school. The driver didn't remember anything out of the ordinary. That left only the remaining kid on the bus.

"A funny car." That was all the child remembered. Deke had gone through all the cars in Elma once again to come up with zilch. Four door family sedans or SUVs were the norm of the day. Dan had no problem putting more of his own time on the investigation but there was nowhere to go. Not even the daily coverage The Buffalo News was giving the story had any payoff either in random calls from the public or getting more manpower on the case.

Dan repeated it to himself as he had done a hundred times before. A man passing through just happens to spot this little boy. Maybe he's stuck behind the school bus and then sees the kid, opens the door. He was reliving the scenario when Cheryl came in.

"Dan, we need something."

"I need more time."

"We're looking bad."

"That's nothing new."

"Don't let me down. This is one the press is loving. A child rape. We're back on CNN again."

Dan started again on the porn sites, hoping for a miracle like a picture of Petey or some kook confessing to the utter blackness of what he'd done or even a fake Santa Claus, like Jess had described. "Come on, be there." Dan prayed. Outside his window the sky was darkening with the threat of snow.

His cell rang. "Come on over. I made sauce."

"On my way, sugar plum." Dan knew he'd regret it but Maggie did a killer spicy sauce with sausage and peppers.

Todd was there. Dan hugged him and Maggie.

"Everything okay?" Maggie gave him the once over and took in the dark circles.

"Almost."

"The hot date?" Todd asked.

"Could be hotter." Dan smiled, "Look, she's a friend at this point."

"As in just a friend. Since when?" Maggie asked.

"I'm starving." Dan changed the topic and Maggie moved them into the kitchen where she had the table set. Dan had had hundreds of dinners over the years with and without Miranda when the boys were growing up. "You need a checkered tablecloth and a violin for this dinner."

"The one good thing I got from Vic, a good sauce recipe. Besides, you and your brother, of course." She smiled at Todd.

"Chianti?" Maggie held the bottle out for Dan.

"No way. I haven't seen one of those in years. Next thing you'll be saving it to put candles in."

"Candles? Gross."

"Before your time, Toddling." Maggie reached over and brushed his hair out of his eyes.

"That was Miranda's idea of décor when I first met her." As soon as he said it they fell silent.

"I had those too.'

"You didn't put away nearly as much of the stuff."

Maggie smiled, "Remember that rug."

"White shag. She actually combed that sucker."

"Filled with Dander's fur."

"That repulsive little animal." Dander was Miranda's small Pomeranian mix.

"Humping me every time I came over." Now Maggie was laughing.

"And I missed all that." Todd said.

"You just don't remember." Maggie answered.

"You must remember some of it." Dan was surprised.

"Sure. My Aunt. Who wouldn't remember?" He left it at that.

This was his family and Dan felt a moment of gratitude.

Todd left to meet some friends. Dan cleared the table. Maggie said, "I'm thinking of doing a Master's."

"Another one?"

"Public health. Maybe I can get off my feet and sit in an office for a change."

"Great. Let me know what I can do."

"I need a change. I'm burnt out. I want to scream at them. Like it's the patient's fault, but you know what, sometimes it is. How can people be so stupid? I had a thirteen- year- old who tried to abort. With a knitting needle. We might as well go back to the coat hanger days." She stacked the dishwasher. "So what about the psychic?"

"She's had a rough time of it. Her husband got custody of her daughter."

"Really? That's not usual."

"She said it was because of the psychic thing."

"Hope so. Did you check out the case?"

"Come on. I believe her. Why wouldn't I? You're too paranoid."

"I'm not the cop."

Dan thought about it for a minute. He hadn't done a check on Jess or her ex. Her divorce would show up on legal records.

On Friday, Jess called. "I'm going to do readings in a bookstore. Do you want to come? They charge 20 dollars. It's not for me, it's for the shop." She made sure to tell him that. "It gives them some extra business and it helps them stay open."

"Sure. What about your daughter?"

"I pick her up Saturday morning. Two weekends in a row. We might actually get to a point where we get along and have some fun."

***

Dan took a deep breath to calm down as he entered the tiny bookstore. There was the smell of incense and small fountains in every corner to appease spirits no doubt or in accordance with Feng Shui. He'd never entered this shop between a newsstand and a bead store on Elmwood Avenue. He spent a minute looking through CD's with pictures of waterfalls. "Can I help you?" A woman came up to him and smiled.

"I'm here for the psychic." He didn't know how else to put it.

"She's in the back, through here. They're getting ready to start." She waited for a moment while Dan opened his wallet. Why did Jess do this? There was something of the snake oil salesman about it.

There were seven chairs set up in a semi-circle. There was only one other man, an elderly gentleman with a cane. Jess introduced herself and explained what she did. Dan just observed for a while. She was connecting well; everyone was looking at her, expectantly. How much was on the level?

Dan could tell just by looking at the old man that he'd likely lost his wife. With the women, he could probably figure out something about each one if he analyzed it long enough. Some sort of loss was most likely what brought them. With all of his own losses it would never have occurred to him to come to such a place to seek answers. Why would a person turn to a psychic?

Once they were settled in, Jess asked him, "May I come to you?" She'd explained that was the protocol, to ask permission from the person the spirit wanted to address and to have a chance to hear the voice of the person she would be doing a reading for.

Dan was taken off guard. "Yes."

"I'm seeing a woman right behind you. She says have a Bloody Mary on her and for God's sake, relax. Does that mean anything to you?"

"Yes." Miranda's last drink of choice had been Bloody Marys. She experimented with fresh horseradish and different hot sauces to make the perfect one.

"She says don't worry, be happy, like the song says."

Miranda hated that song when it came out and couldn't resist making up her own lyrics. "Truck run over your feet. Life can be so sweet. Don't worry. Be happy." Dan shivered.

"And check your brakes."

It was all Dan could do to keep from bursting into tears. He had planned on concentrating on everyone around him and now Jess had brought him memories of Miranda from so long ago they had almost been lost. He couldn't focus on what Jess told anyone else and he still felt shaken as the group was breaking up. He wanted nothing more than to bolt, sit on his favorite chair at home, and down a whiskey as fast as he could.

Jess approached him. "So what'd you think?"

"No words. I think you're good. Whatever it is that you do."

"It was a good group tonight. Nice combination of energy. Sometimes you get the ones who try to trip you up on something like their mother's maiden name. It just doesn't work that way."

"Why do they come then?"

"So the skeptics can say, see, it isn't true. She couldn't see the year I graduated from high school. So would you like dinner? There's a nice place next door; it's Friday, fish fry time."

"This doesn't make you too tired then."

"Less than a day with someone who doesn't keep a record of one goddamn receipt and expects me to come up with the magic solution so they don't get caught by Uncle Sam. Like I said, I felt good energy from all of you in the room."

So now Dan was included in this world and it was starting to feel like it made sense. That was worrying. "Can you see when someone's going to die?"

"Possibly."

He took a deep breath. "I always dream I'm dying. In different ways. Most nights."

"Why?"

"I thought you could tell me."

"I'm not a therapist."

"So you don't see anything."

"No, but get your will ready." Jess laughed at Dan's expression. "Relax, it probably means you experience death. You're a cop; you see things. I think that's pretty normal. The brain could be processing all that you go through in the daytime and saving it up for the night when you're relaxed."

"What about the boy? Do your spirits tell you anything?" Dan wanted to know just who the spirits were, but he didn't go any further.

"I wish they would. I really do."

At a bar down the street, Jess was working on a platter of haddock and fries. Dan's fish was broiled. Jess commented, "That takes the fun out of a fish fry."

"Try it." Dan gave her a forkful.

"Not bad but who says butter is healthier?."

"True. I'd use olive oil and capers, with a bit of tomato.

"So you cook. Now you're secret's out." She gave him a big smile.

"Just enough for survival." Years ago with Miranda he went through a phase of elaborate recipes and dinner parties.

"You don't eat much do you?"

"In theory I'm on a diet."

"Really. Why? You aren't overweight."

"Cholesterol. My knee, the stomach. Now don't get me started or I'll sound like an old coot. But talk to me in ten years. You'll see what I mean. Would you like a drink? Cognac?"

"If you promise to wake me up early."

"At dawn if you like. I'll even make you coffee."

***

Sleep wasn't a problem when Dan wasn't alone. No dreams, no waking up afraid to finish the dream. Dan rolled over to check his clock. It was only seven. What time had Jess gotten up?

He had plans to head out with Todd to Home Depot to pick up some wood for shelves. Todd had been complaining for ages that he didn't have a place for all his books. At that age Dan had cinder blocks and boards but now kids were more demanding. Next he'd be asking for an island in the kitchen.

In the afternoon Dan would go back to work. For years he worked on Saturdays; in fact, weekends were usually busy. Sundays were the days he just couldn't fill after Miranda. With Miranda they were recovery days, waking with a blinding headache, and spending the day lounging and doing nothing more than making a big spaghetti dinner. Later on, there were the mornings she'd wake up and vomit but try to hide it from him.

Then there was the running in his 30's until his knee gave out. All the football he played in high school finally exacted its price. Dan winced whenever he walked down the stairs or God forbid, had to run. Maggie gave him glucosamine which he took when he remembered but didn't feel any effects.

At least Dan could still read a menu without glasses but vanity was getting to him. He should be looking for a woman closer to his own age. Jess might even want more children. Dan shuddered at the thought. A child that could be raped and slaughtered. That was the world he inhabited, a big black hole oozing blood. When he closed his eyes he saw Petey, his pale skin with big black bruises around his neck.

In the middle of his reverie the phone rang. There was a break-in at a mansion near the park. Dan wasn't sure mansion was the right name to call the huge houses that faced the park. The owner hadn't even noticed till he got up in the morning. Those security systems usually kept away all but the most intrepid burglars. Luckily the guy hadn't woken up or it could have been worse. He met Deke and they walked around the grounds. Dan checked the security system. The owner of the house, Everet Jones, said, "I don't understand it. Must have been a short in the system. It's never failed before. It's connected directly to the police station."

"Should be easy enough to see if there were any problems on the grid last night." Dan said.

Deke looked at him and Dan knew they both suspected the whole thing had been staged but that would be up to the insurance investigator to decide. Dan just reported what he saw.

***

Afterwards, he and Deke drove out to an old warehouse near the old train station to check out a complaint about lights. "Deke, remind me again why we're doing this."

"Cheryl doesn't want us to lose touch with the process."

"Or she wants to punish us."

"Nothing on the boy?"

"Nada." Dan had interviewed everyone in school, in the neighborhood, all the construction people, and anyone within miles. No DNA, the bastard was a pro or it was a one-time deal and the guy was extremely lucky. He spotted the kid by chance and just went too far. "So what is it that's supposed to be out here?"

"Breaking and entering. Someone saw a light. Can you fucking believe it?"

They got out and walked around the boarded up building near the tracks. "Imagine what that station must have been like back in the day." Dan stopped for a minute to look at the train station.

"A showpiece. A hundred years ago. Well, there ain't shit here now." Deke pushed open the door to the old wooden outpost. "Could be somebody used it to sleep in."

"In this cold?" The temperature inside was only a degree or maybe two warmer than outside which meant somewhere around 15 degrees. There was a sound of scurrying above them. "Rats, there must be something to gnaw on or they wouldn't be here."

"You going to try that to find out?" Deke pointed to the ladder which had replaced the rotted out staircase.

"Hell, let me play tough guy for a day." Dan climbed up and eased himself carefully on the floorboards. "So far nothing." He shone his flashlight into the darkness and spotted a dark mass in the corner. He crawled over to it and poked around. "Aaah." A man was under the blankets and groaned.

"Got ourselves a live one." He shouted downstairs. "Sir, I'm a detective and you're here on private property."

"So fucking what?" The man grunted.

"You could freeze here."

"My room in the Hilton's being cleaned."

"We can take you to a shelter."

"No way. I been there. You want shit stolen. That's where you go."

Despite the cold open space, the smell of the man was potent, a mix of urine, and booze. For a minute Dan thought about just leaving him but the temperatures were still dropping; he could die. He punched a number on his cell for the office. "Look can you get me a number, someone to pick up a homeless guy who's in a warehouse out in Depew." He was put on hold.

Deke shouted from downstairs. "Hey what you going to do? We ain't got all day."

Dan wasn't sure so he gave the guy a hand up. The man had defecated in the corner, using it as a toilet but his possessions were neatly bound up in a box on a cart. He couldn't imagine how the man had gotten it up the ladder. Valuables for him, that was for sure.

They made it down the ladder, the man, used to being evicted, followed him down without a fuss.

"My cart. Give me my cart." Dan climbed back up and passed the cart down to Deke through the hole where the ladder was.

"So we take him in my car?"

"What else? We can drop him off at the shelter downtown. "What's your name?"

"Timothy Leary." Dan had to laugh.

"Let's go." They got him into the car without a protest. Timothy probably realized it was going to get a whole lot colder in the warehouse.

***

In the late afternoon, Todd rushed up the steps to the front porch carrying six boards. Dan followed behind slowly. "Hey unc, your girlfriend's wearing you out. Better get your ass to the gym."

"Did you ever hear of respecting your elders?" They settled in in front of the television to watch NCAA basketball. Dan was so distracted he couldn't focus on the score or even the teams that were playing.

Chapter Five

Jess called in the evening, "I'm heading up to Avon for an antiques show. How does that sound? Would you like to come?"

"Half that stuff is hot. You can't nail a soul on it though." Dan's idea of what constituted theft had been as rigid as Hammurabi's code, but that had been chipped away over the years. In the end the worst thieves were corporate types who never paid for their crimes or if they did it was in some hotel that passed for a minimum security facility. "A break in and months later the stuff shows up. The dealer may just look the other way."

"Well, I guess that's one thing we won't be doing together." Her voice sounded small.

Dan only wanted what was new, nothing old. He'd worn hand me downs from his cousin, Henry, for years. Henry was now down in Florida selling condos for as long as the market held between hurricanes and housing busts. Maggie remembered all the nieces and nephews and got down to Tampa every winter. Since Jess, the memories were flowing from out of nowhere, flooding his brain. Talking about an antique sale had conjured up Henry.

Or his mother. The long illness had no logic; women weren't supposed to get lung cancer, especially those that never smoked. It was his father who put away a pack of camels every day. Dan smoked until his mom died. Now his father was gone too, not too long after Miranda and right after his second marriage. He barely got a honeymoon out of it. Maybe Dan could remember to send a card this year to his stepmother.

It took his father one year almost to the day after his mother died to marry Stella, his neighbor from West Seneca. Stella was a large, noisy woman who baked coconut cakes and never stopped talking. His mother was quiet and thoughtful; Dan had never really understood the attraction.

Jess wasn't like any of the women he'd known. Jess brought with her the strange world she inhabited.

***

Aaron Clark spent the morning cleaning up his computer files so there wouldn't be a trace left. Then it was just a question of waiting it out. So far there had been not even so much as a question directed to him. The cops didn't have a clue; hadn't they so much as admitted it on the news? His record was clean except for one incident down south and even then, nothing had come of it. He was starting to relax. "Nothing will happen." He repeated it to himself.

***

For the hundredth time, Dan wondered what the hell he was going to do. It was his most important case in a long time and there was nothing to report. He took a deep breath. A surprising number of murders were never solved and this one had the rape to top it off. It was not going to be easily forgotten.

An icicle broke from the roof. The big meltdown would be starting soon. Dan couldn't remember if global warming was supposed to result in an ice age or tropical weather. If this winter was anything to go by, the ice age was well on its way. It was March and there were the first signs winter might end just in time for an early Easter.

When he was a kid his mother had dressed him in a navy blue suit for Easter regardless of the temperature. It was her way of saying enough already to the heavens. Sometimes when she said she couldn't bear one more moment of the winter cold, the crocuses in her garden would come up, pushing their way through the remaining snow. Dan still planted them or rather dug them up and stuck them back in the flower beds every year in homage to her.

Those many years ago his mother had needed something beautiful but instead she got a bad-tempered husband. Her way out had been long and painful. Remembering his mother was like going back to a toothache, probing and poking at a sore spot. At some point the pain would come shooting up the nerve.

***

Dan was celebrating Jess's birthday with Jess and her daughter, Chris. When he was a kid going out to a restaurant was a treat, but now they were used to eating out. This restaurant wasn't particularly special. Dan had a gift to give Jess later and he had sent a bunch of roses to her home. He'd chosen orange roses, thinking it made them more special than red.

"I know all of Dad's friends." Chris announced.

Jess smiled across the table at Dan. "And how about your mother's friends?" Dan couldn't resist.

"Just her girlfriends and well, you, now." They were in a Greek restaurant, a step above the typical diners. "I hate Greek food."

"Since when?" Jess asked.

"Plenty on the menu. Burgers, salads." Dan had been the one to suggest this place thinking it wasn't too stuffy. He noticed Chris wasn't a typical teen; she probably would like stuffy.

"Carla says it's terrible and her mom…"

"Carla's mom still wears Birkenstocks. That's what'll happen to you if you keep listening to her."

Dan ordered salad with chicken, Jess, the moussaka, and Chris, a veggie burger. He got a few points for his diet at least.

Jess called him afterwards to talk. "That wasn't so bad."

"No, she was ok. It's a bad age. 12 going on 20. She's a beautiful girl." And she was; Chris was like a small version of her mother. Jess's genes had won out.

"I hate the clothes. She's 12, not a prostitute. She hasn't gotten her period yet. Most of her friends did at 10 or 11. Imagine."

"Hormones. Maybe what they eat."

"You should watch that with all the chicken you eat."

"I'll grow breasts."

"Don't joke. Thank you for the flowers and the earrings. I love them." The earrings were silver with lapis lazuli.

"I'm glad." Dan had no idea what to get her and ended up in a small jewelry store where Dan described Jess and the owner picked them out.

Dan wasn't sure how to make Chris like him. Kids had it hard when their parents split up; all the emotional upheaval and not really having one place to live. He couldn't imagine it, living with two sets of everything.

His parents had stuck together, most likely out of a sense of duty. Home was okay until the moment his father's key turned in the lock and everyone leapt into action. A drink would be prepared, dinner would be served, and there would be tension until Dan could leave the table to study before something set his father off. It could be the meat was too well done; the potatoes had lumps. There were any number of possible triggers and the night would end up with his father screaming and Maggie answering back while his mother turned pale.

There was tension, and it had been destructive, but he and Maggie turned out ok. Or at least Maggie did. Dan wasn't so sure about himself.

Dan was the only man around for his nephews' lives. He attended all the father son sports banquets at school, with Sean a star wrestler. But there was always the feeling it was never enough, that he was a poor imitation of a dad. Maggie was the optimist, no matter how many of her patients died, or how many of her fears came true. She just kept on no matter what. Dan wished he could just do the same without always analyzing every situation to death.

***

Aaron Clark couldn't get into his car without the sinking feeling he was being followed. Whenever he heard a siren, he jumped. The wait was killing him; he knew stories when the police waited until the killer felt safe to move in and pick him up. "Don't be an ass." he told himself. What happened to that bravado? One minute he'd be convinced they'd never find him and the next, he was shaking in his boots. He looked around to make sure no one was on the street.

The car was bothering him. It stuck out, a dark blue VW. Whatever made him buy such a thing? It wasn't even that great but there was a nostalgia to it. The first car he could afford was an original beetle, old but still functioning. Someone could still be driving it. Now he definitely needed something more nondescript, a car everyone was driving.

"Clark," his neighbor always called him by his last name. He was shoveling. "Should be seeing the last of it."

"It's about time." Aaron told himself if he got into the car quickly, then checked first the rearview mirror, then the side ones, and then tapped the steering wheel three times, he would be safe. There would be no surprises waiting for him.

"Careful now." He told himself on his way to the dealer for a trade-in. The VW's weren't exactly hot sale items but it was time to unload it. Aaron didn't even know why he'd waited so long.

It was like he was watching himself on a movie set, from the outside in. A child outside observing a perfect house with Christmas lights and cookies but never allowed in. He was still that child, someone never allowed in.

Aaron was getting ready to bring it all to a close; he had planned it to be smooth, so no one would notice. The last time in Asheville it hadn't gone so far. That boy was older. Just sex. He told himself, "That's the taboo. Boys like sex. Who's to tell me they aren't sexual?"

The trade at the dealer's was effortless and he didn't care he took a loss. He got into the Honda civic, a silver gray car just like half the cars in the city. The dealer was still taking care of the paperwork but Aaron had the registration in the glove compartment and temporary plates and he had a new car. If he could carry a tune, he would have whistled. There was nothing to worry about. He repeated it over and over to himself.

It wasn't supposed to happen; it was an accident. It was such a little body but it wasn't his fault at all. He could still feel the child's warmth against his body. It fell limp and he could imagine carrying him up to bed and tucking him in, in the joy of that moment. Aaron felt the tears well up in his eyes as he carried the child to his car. But by that point, the boy was dead.

Aaron fiddled with the heat that came up through the leather seat. Those were the extras which he deserved. Why not? Maybe he wouldn't even need to leave. He suppressed a giggle. The new driver of the VW could get into some serious trouble.

***

For the millionth time Dan wondered if an early retirement was possible. He thought about retirement at least a few times every day, more if he was on a hard case. He had twenty-two years on the force, starting just out of school and working hard to pay for the criminal justice degree at the State college. He'd wanted to be a lawyer but there wasn't the money or time. He wished he'd bought more apartments with the money his mother left. Who would have suspected she had socked away thousands just for her children? He'd blown most of it with Miranda, a couple of trips, but mostly on partying. Money or the lack of it defined his life and still left him angry, musing over lost possibilities.

There was the list of things he'd do if he could retire. First, there was a dream of having time to build stuff. Dan had made a couple of simple chairs and a table that now sat in Maggie's living room. That would be part of his perfect life, going down to the basement and working on something tangible, the smell of wood, the smoothness under his hands. The intensity of the longing to be over with it, to stop his life the way it was surprised him. He was scared and a scared cop was the worst possible kind.

***

"She liked you."

"She did?"

"She said, hey, he's pretty cool."

"Quite the compliment." Dan was pleased.

"So remember the antiquing?" Dan had hoped she'd forgotten since she hadn't brought it up in a while. "There's one in Ellicotville."

"They'll still have snow down there. It's been a good ski season."

"Here too in case you haven't noticed."

"It's past being snow. It's just black stuff."

"The show's indoors. Don't worry about that."

"Do you do the e-bay stuff?"

"You found me out. That's my vice. I just buy. Which is worse."

"What do you buy?"

"Purses. I have a thing for bags."

"Definitely a women's thing. The purse is a symbol."

"Yeah, and everything else is a penis."

"Do you want to have dinner with us?"

Dan wasn't sure it was a good idea so soon after the first meeting. Jess only saw her daughter every other weekend after all. "Sure." He debated what to bring, but most kids had everything these days. He opted for some chocolates.

***

Chris answered the door without saying anything. "Mother," she called.

Jess came and gave him a kiss. "Chocolates. Mmmm. Thank you."

"What are you making?"

"Pasta. I probably shouldn't considering you said Maggie was such a good cook."

"It smells great." He followed her into the kitchen. Miranda always had a bottle of wine open in the kitchen. Inspiration she called it. She'd been a great cook or maybe he just drank so much he thought so. Jess was neat; the kitchen spotless. Dan opened a bottle of wine. "Chris doesn't want to help." He teased.

"No."

Dan resisted the urge to taste the tomato sauce. "Does it have meat?"

"God forbid with Chris. It's marinara."

"It looks pretty rich."

"Thanks."

"I mean thick for a marinara." He tasted it.

"It's just a sauce."

"Do you have any basil?"

"No."

"I can throw a bit of this wine into it."

"I'm making this."

"Sorry."

"You're lucky I didn't put hot peppers in there."

Dan laughed. "Parmesan. You must have parmesan.'

"Check the fridge."

He found a round container of grated cheese that looked fake.

"Chris, dinner."

They sat at the dining room table. Dan tried, "How'd your basketball team do?"

"Second in the league so far."

"Excellent."

Dan tried a few more questions that she was polite enough to answer but didn't offer any more information.

As soon as she ate a little bit, Chris asked. "Can I be excused?"

"Did you eat enough?"

"Mother, it tastes awful. I don't know how you can mess up pasta."

When Chris left the room, Dan felt his body relax. Finally when Jess spoke she said, "She'll be telling her friends how bad a mother I am. She can't even make pasta."

"It's a long process. Don't worry." Dan doubted he could ever win Chris over. She was just getting over her mother's divorce.

"She's not much better when it's just the two of us you know. So, it's not you." Jess got up to clear the table.

"I'll do it. Sit." Dan stacked the dishwasher, relieved to have a few minutes alone. His nephews were never like that but Maggie hadn't dated much after the divorce. In fact, she still didn't. He rejoined Jess in the living room where she was staring straight ahead. "It's okay." He tried to cheer her up. "Want to watch TV?" They sat like an old married couple flipping through the channels.

So first Chris liked him and now she didn't. It was the prerogative of a twelve-year-old. He knew he should call upstairs for her to come down, but he hesitated. Then his conscience won out. "Come on down, Chris." He shouted it in an imitation of The Price is Right though she was probably too young for it to mean anything at all. At least she didn't have a TV in her room. "We'll let you choose."

Dan wondered what the ex was like besides the obvious fact that he had bucks, given the house and Chris's designer clothes. This was not a girl who had to do chores and work for an allowance.

Chris plopped down on the floor, first holding out her hand for the remote control. Flipping through the channels, she found a remake of Sabrina with Harrison Ford. Jess complained, "All that romance will warp your mind."

Dan started going through his pockets for an antacid. Jess only had aspirin in her medicine cabinet. Lately, Maggie was trying to get him to use ginger instead. It didn't matter since he didn't have either with him. He sat silent, his stomach churning acid.

***

Early Monday morning Dan was watering the Ficus in the corner of his office. It had taken over the corner and was growing taller. "What'd you do, talk to it?" Everyone who came into his office commented. The plant had originally occupied the reception desk when Dan rescued it from a certain death. He found some of the strands of tinsel he'd thrown on it for Christmas still clinging to the pot. Coffee mug in hand, Dan started with the boy's file again.

There was a man asking to see him. There hadn't been any leads so Dan was hoping this guy had something. "John Sterner," the man held out his hand. "I was down in Florida. My brother died and I had to go down and take care of things. I didn't even turn on the tube. You can't imagine the mess he left behind. He was one of those guys who didn't throw out a thing, not a single piece of junk mail in the last fifteen years. Publishers Clearing house and all. Kept thinking he'd throw out something important. Then when I got back, my neighbor got to talking about Petey. Horrible thing to happen. Nice little kid too."

Dan didn't want to interrupt the man but a simple piece of information could be lost in all this talk. "So is there something specific you wanted to talk about?"

"The car. I saw a strange car up that way. I remember the day cause that was the day after I found out about my brother. I spent the whole day trying to make reservations to get a flight out. I was packing and I opened up the front door to see if it had stopped snowing and I saw it. One of those new VW bugs, blue. Don't see too many of those around. Don't think they're very practical up here. I had one of the originals so it made me smile." Mr. Sterner was in his 70's and with white hair, and an air of Santa Claus to him. "I heard that sound of a car trying to get out of the snow, revving up the motor you know."

"Did you see who was driving?"

He shook his head. "It was too far. My eyesight's not what it used to be."

"Do you live alone?"

"I have an aid who comes in a couple times a week, that's all. Meals on wheels too. Glad they come out this far. My brother used to try to get me to come down to Sarasota with him. I was born right in the house I still live in. My people raised horses out here back when there were still farms." Mr. Sterner took a deep breath and wheezed. "Got some lung problems. Smoked too long. I just couldn't quit. You don't smoke, do you?"

"Used to. My mother died of lung cancer." Dan didn't know why he offered this piece of information.

"Nasty habit. Still want one most days though."

"And the car." Dan urged him back on track.

"It was after three because I was on the phone cancelling my aid and the meals and trying to line up a ride to the airport. I take a green pill then. Stacey lines them all up for me with the hour I need to take them. And then I got out my suitcase."

The car was the first lead, tenuous though it might be. A car like that wouldn't be hard to track down."Mr. Sterner, why did you wait so long to tell us? It's been weeks."

"Like I said, I was busy down there. Don't watch much TV anyway and I didn't know until I got back and my neighbor came over the other day."

"Thank you."

Dan showed him out and immediately got to work. The VW bug was not a common model. He checked the DMV for all owners. While he waited for the lists to come through, he worked on another cup of coffee. Immediately he regretted it as an acid bubble formed in his chest.

Deke stuck his head in, "Anything up?"

"Could be a big fat zero but there might be a lead. Could be something." He tried hard not to say sumptin', like Deke would.

"Good thing. How about a beer tonight after work?"

"Sure." Deke was his closest friend so he had to make an effort though he just wanted to go home and sit in his chair with the TV on. "Just waiting now for the lists."

"How many blue VW bugs are there in town? What the hell is that color? Midnight blue?" Deke leaned over to see the models on Dan's computer screen. "That's not a car, that's some shit-mobile."

"I looked it up. Two blues, galactic blue and blue lagoon." Dan didn't want to miss the expression on Deke's face. "Didn't you ever have a beetle?"

"Ugly back then and worse now. Hitler mobiles."

Dan changed the subject. "How long till retirement?" It was their shared fantasy since neither could though they didn't stop talking about it.

"6 years, 7 months, and 15 days. I'm heading right down to North Carolina, the outer banks." He stopped for a minute. "But with the kids it ain't gonna happen. You know how now everything has to be a brand name now. Hell, I used to cut the red tag off my Levi's just to get that dam thing off."

"Where's Clarisse?"

"East side. A shooting last night."

The list came on the screen. Dan hit print. "Keep your fingers crossed." He got a VW that had been traded in over a month ago. "Thank you, Jesus. Let's go."

They got to the dealership out on Sheridan Drive. It was a busy time of day with customers coming in after work and salespeople all over the lot. Dan headed to the office. On the way he saw a dark blue car sitting right on the lot. Dan punched in the license number. A man in a suit intercepted him. He was either eager or sales were slow.

"Just got that. Cute car."

Dan flashed his ID. "Tell me about the owner."

"He wanted a more sedate model. I wasn't surprised. People get tired of a car that's so different. The color isn't bad, a nice blue. They got it in red and a kind of mint green."

"Was he in a hurry to sell it?"

"Not particularly. He didn't bargain much but then he was getting a good car, one of last year's at a good price. He understood he had to take a loss. His car's a couple of years old."

"So you remember him. How old would you say he was?"

The salesman frowned. "Not too young, not too old. You know I can't tell anymore. I guess, under 40."

"How tall was he?"

Terez Peipins • 72

Dan already knew the answer. "Medium. Kind of a typical guy. He was friendly enough. Brown hair. Brown eyes, I think."

"Anything else you could tell me about him?"

"He was itchy. He was scratching his hands."

They were a couple of steps behind this guy. "Can I take a look at the receipt?"

"Come on. I've got it in the office. We keep everything of course."

Dan needed to get the car checked out but it wasn't going anywhere and by now it wasn't going to be holding any evidence. "What condition was the VW when he brought it in?"

"Well, you saw it out there. Excellent. We do a once over when we get them. Clean them and vacuum the inside, check out the trunk, that sort of thing. But really it was spotless. Even smelled clean, one of the guys said so. A lot of the vehicles we get stink. Smoke, food, God knows what and you don't want to ask. But not that one."

***

The sales staff was waiting in the warmth until they had to step out to help customers. The showroom held two Hondas. Dan glanced at them. "Is this like the new car?"

"Same color as the one he got. It's nice, isn't it? Four door sedan. Pretty standard. But the guy got it with some extras, leather seats, heated. We had one right here."

Dan looked over the papers and copied down the address. Deke was still looking at the VW. "Bingo."

"Finally." Deke set out to inspect the car, bagged a few fibers from the carpet in the trunk to compare with any on the kid's clothes and they headed out to the address on the receipt.

When they got to the Amherst apartment, Dan laid on the buzzer. And older man standing by the stoop said."He left a couple of weeks ago. Moved right out."

"Say where he was going?"

The man shook his head. "Don't know."

"Can we ask you a couple of questions?" Dan asked.

"Yes." He led them upstairs to his apartment. "Aaron in trouble? We were neighbors for two years." Dan let him continue. "Quiet guy, that one, maybe a bit odd."

"Why?" Dan asked.

"Computer guy. A nerd, right? Just that, work and computers."

Dan glanced over at Deke who gave him a nod. "Did he have any contact with kids?"

"No. He used to yell at the ones who'd play in front of his windows, said he couldn't concentrate. First floor you get all the street noise. It's usually pretty quiet but summertime, kids will be kids. They got skateboards now."

"Did he work at home?"

"No, he went somewhere every day."

Dan had to get a warrant to open up the place though if he was as thorough as with the car, there wouldn't be much left to find. "Did he get a new car?"

"Matter of fact he did. Had that VW and got a regular one. Guess he got tired of it. Say, this doesn't have anything to do with that kid?"

"We don't know."

"Seemed like a decent guy. Shoveled me out more than once."

"Thank you, Mr."

"Marshall."

"Here's my card. Call me if he comes by or you remember anything else." Dan doubted Aaron Clark was anywhere around here at this point.

"I always wanted to hear that from a cop." Mr. Marshall grinned.

"They all weird or what?" Deke asked as they left.

"They watch too much TV. Nothing is as real as that." Dan started ringing the other four bells. Mr. Marshall came out again. "They're all still at work."

"Thank you. So now what. We have to wait for the court order."

"We'll grab dinner around here. No sense in driving back to town."

Chapter Six

This was the part of a case that Dan liked the best. There was a flurry of activity with a lead. There was a purpose, dealing with something that was bigger than all of them. It was like digging in a tunnel without any hope of getting out and finally glimpsing a faint ray of light.

Like the car, the apartment had been cleaned up. Clark hadn't rushed off anywhere. He'd taken his time. It was a standard rental as far as Dan could tell. The building was new without any of the distinctive details that marked the older houses in the city.

Dan picked up some threads from the wall to wall carpeting just in case it matched anything on the kid. He looked around the bathroom to see if anything had escaped Clark's careful exit. He got down on his knees and groped the floor near the tub and found a hair. "All right." He carefully placed in a plastic bag.

When they got back to the station, they got to work after dropping the samples off in the forensic lab.

"Edgar, are the boy's clothes still down there?" Dan didn't even need to identify the name.

"Evidence. I can get them."

"We got this." He handed Edgar the plastic bags from the car and the apartment. "Can you see if there are any matches on the fiber and the hair? Something the kid may have picked up." Dan paused a minute. "Do you remember any stains on the clothes? Could you check them out for any signs of hand cream?"

"This case finally moving?"

"That's what we're hoping." Dan smiled at the older man. Edgar was lanky and pale, but then everyone was in winter. He'd been doing his job for a long time, long before the TV shows focused on forensic science and turned it into something exciting.

So far they had all the basic information on him. Aaron Clark was 38, average height, brown hair, brown eyes, one previous arrest with no prosecution. His hair was cut very short, most likely to mask balding. He was an IT person at a local bank. 38 years of life without leaving too much of a mark.

Dan looked up from the files as Deke asked. "A psycho? What about his family?"

"Mother died when he was ten. Lived with his aunt until he went to school. She died last year."

"Let's see what else we can dig up. I'll see if I can get the school records on him."

"Something must have snapped." Now it was just a question of getting a match on a hair or fiber from the kid's clothing. Dan was keeping his fingers crossed.

The VW was spotless. Those TV crime shows always said bleach was the ultimate cleanser, removing all clues and in this case the car had been scrubbed clean. The dealership had just removed the last of any evidence.

It would be just a question of tracking Aaron Clark down based on Mr. Sterner having seen the car. More evidence would certainly help but they'd lost too much time already. With the new car model and plates, they'd send out an APB and it would be over.

Dan suspected that would be too easy. This guy knew to get out right at the perfect moment. Plus, he had a head start on them.

Aaron Clark had been arrested by the police in Asheville, North Carolina. "What the hell was he doing there?" Dan asked himself; that was an artsy town in the mountains. He checked the records and found that no one had pressed charges. Clark had been working with a Head Start group of adolescents ten years ago. Details usually didn't keep for that long.

Dan called the local Asheville Precinct and asked to be put through to one of the veteran officers, someone who had been there ten years before. Dan himself would be one of those.

A Southern drawl came over the line. "Sergeant Winsley here."

Dan explained the whole situation and got Winsley's attention when he mentioned the murder. "I'm looking for anything you might have on Aaron Clark."

"That was quite a while ago. I can check the records but it rings a bell. We're up in the mountains here and we get a lot of summer campers. You know, the usual, hiking and camping, taking kids on these treks to build, what the hell is it? Now they call it team building skills. Back then it was taking kids who were on a bad path and trying to set them straight."

"Do you remember Aaron Clark?" Dan couldn't picture Clark as the outdoors type of guy.

The Sergeant got busy on his computer. "I remember him. He was scared stiff. Some kids accused him of sexual abuse."

"How many kids were involved?"

"Two. But I think the one was just there as support for his buddy."

"How old were they?"

"Fourteen."

Was there any evidence?" Dan flashed on Petey's body.

"It never got that far. There was nothing concrete at all. That's why the case got dropped. We were never sure if it was some kids wanting to get back at their counselor or if something did happen. We got in a psychiatrist but these kids were in too tough a position themselves to press charges. Some trouble with the law, robbery, that kind of thing, last thing they needed was this. Maybe they just wanted to scare him."

"Or it was worse than all that for them to even protest."

"Nothing came of it."

"Except this."

"Now that's a bad situation."

Dan wanted to answer no kidding. Instead he thanked the Sergeant for his help and asked for the records to be sent over. He had the name of the camp and the director to call.

***

Maggie called him, "Hey, Dan are you okay? I've been calling for days."

Dan tended to lay low when he got busy on a case. "Just working."

"That's a good thing, isn't it?"

"Hope so. How are you?"

"Great. I'm leaving for Tampa tomorrow. Sunshine, remember what that is?"

"It's that yellow light isn't it?" The sun hadn't so much as peeked out from behind the clouds in four days. "Visiting the cousins?"

"Yup. Beach time. It's about 85 down there. I've been following weather.com for days."

"Stop, I can't stand it. Do you need a ride to the airport?"

"Todd's taking me. Should I bring you some oranges?"

"How 50's of you. I'd like that. I can't remember the last time I had some vitamin C." At the moment he was drinking his coffee out of one of Maggie's Florida souvenirs. This one had a shark with "Send more tourists, the last ones were delicious" on it.

"Next time you come with me."

"I'd like that."

"They always ask about you. So check up on Todd, will you?"

"Of course. I'll even cook."

"Invite Jess too. That could be interesting."

"So have a good trip."

"One more thing."

"Winnie?"

"Yes."

"I'll bring her over." The last time the dog stayed with him he had to race home after work to take her out and then she would stop right in the middle of the sidewalk, refusing to budge.

"Love you."

"Love you too."

***

The transcripts of the camp kids' testimonies and Aaron Clark's interrogation lay on Dan's desk. Dan could see how the case never went to trial. The two boys were city kids stuck in a camp in the mountains. They accused Aaron Clark of making them suck his penis. The boys were fourteen but small for their ages. Tough city kids. Aaron Clark was not in that league. Would he even have approached them or was it the other way around? Dan did a check on them and came up with nothing. No recent records so whatever petty crimes had sent them to the camp had not turned into something more serious.

Aaron had answered all the questions with as few words as he could get away with. The defense's tactic was to make the boys look guilty. Dan read the transcript.

"Did you have any type of sexual relations with Jackie Hunt and Jeremy Blackwell?"

"No, I did not." It was their word against his.

Dan wondered if Aaron Clark was innocent. These boys had nothing in common with Petey Jackson.

He found the camp director, who was still down in Asheville. Dan explained why he was calling. It took a few moments for Alex to remember. "Of course." He finally said. "Clark was a nerdy guy. Not meant for this kind of camp."

"How did he end up there?"

"College credit. We were supposed to have computers but the funding never came through. Clark knew nothing about the mountains but then neither did the kids."

"Was he guilty of abusing Hunt and Blackwell?"

"Who knows? They weren't the nicest kids."

***

With the plate numbers and a description of Clark's new car out all over the country, something should have come up by now. Nothing had been leaked to the press so Clark wouldn't know.

What Dan wanted to do now was put his head down on his desk and take a breather. The phone snapped him out of his mini nap. Jess reminded him about the antique sale in Auburn. Dan felt guilty about not going to the last one, so he said, "I'll go."

"You must really want to see me."

"Yup. Is Junior coming?"

Jess got defensive. "Why is that a problem?"

"Not at all."

"She hates old stuff. Her Dad will be buying her the latest of whatever it is she may want."

Dan thought, "At least we've got that in common. Of course, my Dad didn't do any buying."

***

Jess's car was the same color as Aaron Clark's. The same color as thousands on the road. Gray was popular and didn't stand out. Dan hadn't slept well and was feeling groggy. Flashes of the boy in the snow, dreaming of the phone ringing, and if that weren't enough, the death dream, this time in the guardrail version, all conspired to keep him from a deep sleep.

"All the good stuff is gone early." Jess said. That explained why they were setting off at six AM on a weekend.

They didn't speak much. "I'll stop at the reservation for gas." They pulled up to a small shop on the Seneca reservation. Dan looked around for snacks but the best he could do was a diet coke from a machine. Jess came back with a couple of cartons of Marlboro Lights, "For my neighbor." She put them in the trunk. "Didn't you have breakfast?"

Dan shook his head. "I had a rough night so I was just finally in a deep sleep when you called."

Jess hesitated. "If we stop it defeats the purpose of starting so early."
"Don't worry. This is clearing the cobwebs. They'll have something in there." He held up the can and went into the convenience store where he picked up a box of Little Debbie brownies, a vague memory from childhood coming back when he looked at the box with the drawing of a little girl on it.

"Those look good." Jess commented.

"You're kidding. Here, I'll unwrap one for you. Individually wrapped. More for the landfill."
"They're meant for kids' lunches."

"I bet Chris would never eat that. God, you're even cheerful this morning. What time did you go to bed?"

"Early. I was beat."

The show was held in a local grammar school. They parked, and Dan went off to find a restroom leaving Jess to her bargain hunting. When he came out, he couldn't find her. It was just before eight but the place was already packed. The gym and cafeteria were filled with table after table or every imaginable object. Dan didn't get the appeal of it all.

There was a table covered with old signs which looked like they may have been stuck on barns ages ago.

"Aren't these great?" Jess motioned him over and spoke in a low voice.

"Where do they come from?"

"An old train station near Attica. There was a line years ago, the Attica Arcade. Chris took the train on a class trip a couple of years ago."

Dan followed Jess around until he finally saw something that appealed to him, baseball cards. There were cards of all the heroes of his childhood, Johnny Bench, Pete Rose and Dale Murphy.

Jess had picked up tin boxes ."Look," she was excited, "They were used for oatmeal. Aren't they great? Well, I think that's it for me. How about you? Is there anything else you'd like to look at?"

Dan shook his head, thrilled it was over, and feeling like a reprieved child. Jess went on, "We can have lunch. It's early, but you didn't have breakfast."

Dan all but raced to the car. "This is definitely not your thing. I'll remember." Jess smiled at him.

"I had to give it a try."

"But why don't you like it?"

"Too close to home. I once spent six months trying to recover stolen goods from a robbery in the city. I went back and forth all over the state. I even learned about Shaker furniture." He didn't add he thought he could make it himself if he just had more time.

They stopped at a classic style diner. Dan ordered an omelet with home fries. Jess had pancakes and sausages. Dan looked at it remembering the last time he'd eaten a sausage at the Italian festival in the summer. He was trying to remember a time when food had no digestive consequences.

"Maggie's in Florida."

"Do you ever go with her?"

"I should one of these days. Usually, I'm busy this time of year."

"I used to travel a lot when I was married. We even took a cruise to the Bahamas."

"Did you like that?"

"What's not to like?"

For Dan the idea of spending time trapped on a big boat full of people was hell itself. "It seems artificial."

"Don't you get enough reality?"

"Good point. Miranda and I visited Puerto Rico. She spoke Spanish pretty well."

"Don't you?"

"Basic stuff like Como estas? La gran chingada. That's about my limit."

"So you like cultural vacations."

"I'd like to go to Costa Rica one day. See the rain forests, that sort of thing." He had brochures at home, but he had never traveled alone. It didn't hold much appeal for him. Dan's headache and general fuzziness were beginning to fade after his third cup of coffee.

"You've been really busy lately. I'm glad you could come out with me."

"Can't really talk about it."

***

Jess dropped Dan off at the station. He told himself for the thousandth time his job wasn't compatible with a life.

Deke came into the office as Dan was leaning over his desk doubled over his desk with the acid burning in his chest. "That's it, bro. I'm cutting you off the coffee. You're going to start on the green tea."

"I hate tea. That's the worst. It tastes like grass."

Deke smiled, "it's good for you." He never said boss but it was like his sentences ended with the word unsaid.

"What are you doing here? Go home, it's Sunday."

"I'm out of here. Just catching up with some paperwork. What about you? Don't usually see you here on Sunday."

"I just spent the morning antiquing. Believe me, I'd rather be here."

"Antiquing? Is that like a real word? You must really like her. So, what is that she's into?"

"Prints and signs."

"Could be worse, some people collect junk like chamber pots. Is her house full of that shit?"

Dan shook his head, "Nothing. I haven't seen any boxes or junk lying around. Who knows, maybe her basement may be full of shit or maybe she sells it on e-bay."

"People making a living selling crap. You'd think she'd pick up vibes handling that old shit."

Dan laughed. He started through the sheaf of papers on his desk, left there since Friday. No Honda, no stolen vehicles, no airplane tickets. Nothing new. He checked the internet again at some of the sites he was monitoring. It made him queasy though most of the sites were discreet at least for the initial contact. By the time he finished it was already seven. He called Jess.

"You're still at work?" She was surprised.

"I'm getting ready to leave. Hey, what do you do with all the stuff you buy?"

"The signs are for my mom. She has a shop and the prints I frame."

"I hadn't noticed."

"They're on the walls of the living room. I can't believe you didn't notice."

"It just doesn't register for me. House stuff I don't notice. Not when I'm not on duty."

"And you're a cop. You're supposed to notice everything. That's your job. So what was I wearing today?"

"Blue sweater, thick wool with a kind of braided pattern, jeans, boots. You looked good. Did I tell you? And you were wearing a new perfume. It smelled like some kind of vegetable."

"Green tea."

"Deke just told me I should be drinking that." Dan stopped himself from saying it was a sign. "Do I pass?"

"Yes."

"Can I see you next week?"

"You're the busy one. Give me a call when you've got time."

When he hung up, Dan punched in his nephew's number. "Todd, what do you want, Chinese, or pizza?"

"Pizza."

"Okay, but you've got to come get me."

They settled into a booth in an old pizzeria in Todd's neighborhood. Todd ordered extra hot Buffalo wings. Dan cringed and ordered a calzone, with what he hoped would be acid absorbing dough.

Todd passed him the basket. "Try one."

"Can't do it. I think you have to be 20 to digest those."

"You want to have a drink after we eat?"

"Got an early morning. You hear from your mother yet?"

"No, she forgot she has kids."

Dan smiled, remembering a time with Miranda when there was a possibility of having children. Maggie lived for her kids. Deke was the same. He had one child with dyslexia who was first in his class no less, and a daughter who ruled his life.

***

All those years ago, Miranda had waited for him with the news. As soon as he stepped in the door, she hugged him and said, "Guess what? I'm pregnant."

He hugged her back though things weren't going well and a baby wouldn't set things straight. "I'm so glad, darling."

Miranda was so happy she didn't notice Dan's hesitant response. It was a high that lasted three months until it bled away. Dan had worried the entire time the baby would have fetal alcohol syndrome. He'd read about the signs like smaller eye openings and even learned the word philtrum, the vertical groove between the nose and the upper lip. In a child with the syndrome the philtrum was undeveloped and from then on, Dan then kept a lookout for it. He suspected the problem was more widespread than most people thought.

Miranda hadn't been trying to get pregnant which meant she had been her usual several drink a day self when she found out. When she lost the baby, he was almost relieved but not quite. He had begun to believe the dream of a happy family and that was something he couldn't allow.

Miranda, of course, got depressed. She wasn't drinking excessively so one would notice, just steadily. She started as soon as she got home, hours before Dan and finished around midnight, never falling down, just a bit unsteady on her feet or wobbling on her way up to bed. They used to joke about it. "I'll have to put you to bed." And Dan would. Before he made detective, he'd managed to keep up with her. In fact, drinking seemed normal to him.

"Hey unc, where are you?"

"Thinking about Miranda."

"You've got the memory of an elephant. What about Jess?" Todd raised his eyebrows.

"Her daughter doesn't like me."

"Turn on the charm."

"It doesn't work with a twelve-year-old. So what's up with your brother these days?"

"No news. I can't track him down."

Dan smiled. "Tell me about it. Sean will be running the world."

Todd just hadn't found his way yet. He had even asked Dan about joining the force which was flattering, but he had told his nephew, no way. He couldn't bear the idea of worrying about Todd. He had enough on his plate with his own ever present death fears.

Thanks to Maggie, Todd got paramedic training and a job on the ambulance squad. He was holding up though Dan didn't think it was the right job for such a sensitive guy. Todd just wasn't very ambitious. He was into registering people to vote and joining a group that planted trees in bad neighborhoods. He spent a few hours every week at a homeless shelter.

"Is Sean coming home this summer?"

"I guess not. He's pretty busy with school; plus, he's got a new girlfriend."

"Isn't he coming for a visit at least?"

"I think he might have but Mom is in Florida. He'll show up for a week before exams. He always does. He says he needs a week in a quiet place."

A week was about all Maggie could handle. Sean came home expecting the world to stop for him. That meant meals served and the quiet he needed, a given. There was more of Maggie in Sean; he was directed. Todd had always been Dan's favorite, softer than his brother, who already had law school and a political career mapped out. Sean never let doubts creep in.

Dan looked across the table at his nephew. Todd was the only person in the world who filled him with a sense of hope. When he got home, he put on his old Coltrane record, "A Love Supreme" and felt it.

Chapter Seven

In the morning, when Dan got to his office, a report was sitting on top of the usual pile of papers on his desk. A car was stopped outside of Amherst, Massachusetts with the telltale plates. It wasn't a Honda but an old Buick. "Changed the plates." By now he'd probably done it a few times. That is if he wasn't already on a plane. How did he know? Intuition again?" It had taken the old man to get them on track. "If he hadn't been in Florida, Clark would have been behind bars already."

Dan stared at Clark's job photo ID. Talk about not standing out, Aaron Clark could have been a spy in the cold war. He was medium everything- height, weight, skin color- nondescript, eyes brown, hair brown.

Dan headed to the bank where Clark had worked; Deke and Clarise had already been, but today only two of the work group were there. The IT department was down in the basement, made up of three men and a woman, all in their 30's. It was a job without much of a future since outsourcing had hit the industry hard.

The woman was the first to look up from her computer. "Can't take too much time. They monitor practically every minute we're on. They dock us if the breaks are too long." Dan introduced himself.

"I'm Nicki. We worked together but I didn't know Aaron all that well. We already told the police all this."

"Did you ever socialize with him?"

"We went out for a drink Fridays, whoever was here, just to Connor's around the corner. It's a tradition; we always have. It's our way to start the weekend."

"Is there anything you noticed about him? Anything you could comment on?"

"He wasn't a big drinker. Not like some of us. A couple of beers and he's ready to go home. Oh, and he started taking the bus a while ago. He said something about having problems with his car, but I just figured he's trying to save some money."

"Anything special about him physically?"

"He had really dry skin. He was always using creams, like women do. He used to keep them in his drawer."

It was the second time his skin was mentioned. Dan continued, "What was he like to work with?"

"We don't get much time to chat. We sometimes have to go upstairs and clean up people's messes. You can't believe what they can do to a simple desktop. Usually we're plugged in, answering calls or fixing problems. It's a big building with lots of computers. This is the national headquarters. You know, Aaron seemed pretty normal to me. But maybe I'm not a good judge of people."

"How long have you known him?"

"We started the same time here so it's been about two years."

"Were you friends?"

She shrugged. "Not really. Like I said he sometimes had drinks on Fridays with everybody. That's about it. I didn't really know anything about him."

"Do you ever see him outside of work?"

"Only once. Charlie's wedding and Aaron needed a date."

"And how did that turn out?"

"We didn't spend much time together. He was doing magic tricks for the kids." She noticed Dan's expression, "Not a good thing, huh."

Considering the gravity of such a crime, Dan didn't understand why none of the bank staff seemed especially upset that a workmate was suspected of murder and rape. None of them gave much information about Clark. Did he inspire some kind of loyalty or was it because there wasn't much to say about the guy? Dan could only hope it wasn't because everyone was so jaded with the horrors shown on TV every night that the nasty reality right in front of them had no impact.

***

Aaron Clark's heart was pounding. He got off the bus at Port Authority to the smell of burnt rubber and gasoline. It was his first time in New York. Under his down jacket his t-shirt stuck to his back. Long ago he had dreamt of coming to New York back when his aunt was alive. But that city was different; this one was grey and smelly. He could have been in an underground parking garage anywhere except this one was enormous.

Life could have been different, and not just now with what happened. In his fantasies Aaron would be free of the brain fever; he'd have the possibility of falling in love. Love could be something different; something that didn't hurt. He read about those characters in the novels his aunt collected and he developed a fondness for. His aunt Claire bought them in stacks and except for the covers, the stories were almost identical, a woman and a man falling madly in love, overcoming all obstacles and distance to be together.

Those books were so far removed from life that he couldn't believe his aunt would read such things. As he got older, he looked for something else, to find a point of comparison, to see if there could be anyone who was worse off, anyone who had it worse.

First, it was on Oprah with the parade of abused men and women confessing their sorry stories and then the media was flooded with them. Everyone was jockeying positions to spill the unthinkable. Even then, he was unable to speak or put into words any of what he lived, not even to himself. He knew his stories were worse than anything on TV.

Once his Aunt Claire, sitting with the newspaper on her lap and the TV on to its usual Jeopardy episode, turned to him and said, "Your mother had it hard.

Your granddad wasn't the kindest man." When he didn't respond she went on, "I was older but all I wanted to do was to get out when I could. Maybe I abandoned her."

That was all that she said. Aaron sometimes tried to read between the lines of that conversation. It was what he held onto, that his mother had not been to blame." A victim, was that what she was in the end?" he asked. He wanted to believe it; then it meant that he could love her. She was his only candidate for him to love though she was long gone.

He saw them at the bank sometimes; people with their perfect lives. That was a life he was never allowed.

***

Aaron called the bank just to make sure they had his last paycheck. That was when he found out the police had been around; the guys made it sound as if it were a joke but that didn't fool Aaron. That's when he had ditched the Honda and started taking buses. First he changed the plates and sold the car in Albany on his way downstate. Now all he needed was a chance to think straight. Coming to New York City was a good move; he could get anywhere from New York.

See America, go Greyhound and leave the driving to us. Sure. If the short haul from Albany to New York was any indication, he'd never make it through a longer trip. The bus was smelly and his companions a sad lot.

Money was becoming a problem. He'd been withdrawing as much money as he could over the last couple of months but carrying a lot of cash in a big city was not a very smart idea. He really wasn't made for this; he couldn't stop his heart from racing. He felt it would burst out of his chest.

All he wanted was to go home and plug in his real computer, the one he had to give up, not the little laptop in his backpack. "Stupid kid. Stupid, stupid little kid. Look what you've done." Aaron hit his fist against his open palm. He took a deep breath and tried to calm himself down. "Relax. You're almost clear."

***

"New York? An ATM?" Dan looked down at the information in front of him.

"How many people there in that city?"

"I don't even know anymore. I used to know that kind of shit in high school. Maybe around ten million." Deke answered.

"It's a good place to hide or to get somewhere else."

"Aren't they checking his ID?"

"Not if he's paying cash. If he uses the card to buy things for small amounts, he doesn't even need to sign."

"How much he take out?"

"The maximum."

"He's not getting far."

"Cheap flights. Where would you go?"

"I'd sit tight. A big city. It could take a while to track him down."

"Let's say he's not a big city guy. He's scared." Dan said.

Deke said, "The guy knows how to cover his trail." Deke went on, "All those abuse cases piling up. What about that little town in Wyoming County? Two priests in less than two years. Damn perverts, all of them."

"How'd we get on to priests?"

"A pervert is a pervert."

"Even if he's a priest, you mean."

***

Aaron Clark had been careful except for the ATM. He hadn't been on the Internet as far as they could tell. There had been no record of him on any of the sites they'd checked but then again he would know how to cover his tracks.

If people's sexual oddities were exposed half the world would be out of the orbit of normal and that's precisely what Dan found checking the internet. There was regular kinky stuff which while it could be distasteful, there didn't seem to be much harm in consenting adults pissing on each other. He'd considered himself someone who didn't shock easily but when he had checked the 50th site with kids in every conceivable position doing what he didn't want to imagine, he'd just about plunged into despair.

"My son's making his first communion." Deke said.

"He's that age."

"Too much church. That's what I say."

"Can't hurt. The golden rule and all that. What do you want, him playing with snakes and talking in tongues?" Dan teased him.

Cheryl interrupted them as she came into the office. Deke had been the first to complain about a woman boss but she had proved herself to be a fair player and a great administrator who had their backs. "So what exactly have you got?"

Dan had had a crush on Cheryl, even if she got what was supposed to be his job. Then again, everyone had in the beginning. She had curly brown hair and freckles, and she was slightly overweight, what was once called plump. She disguised it well in her dark pantsuits which made her 5'4 frame look taller. She even managed to disguise the fact she was an optimist, a danger in the police department where sarcasm and bad moods reigned. She looked like a normal everyday mom and that had the effect of a mother meting out punishment to naughty children.

"Well, hello. I haven't seen you in days. How are you? The kids?" Dan tried a different tactic.

She smiled. "Mark is playing the sax."

"All right." If Dan remembered right Mark was her ten-year-old. Usually he could keep the names of the offspring of his workmates straight but as the years were passing by so fast, he could barely keep up.

There was a whiteboard in the corner of his office. It squeaked as Dan pulled it closer to the desk. He pointed to the center. "Finally, we got some signs of life. New York. He used an ATM. We've got a search going on for him."

"So how did he figure out we were onto him?"

"No one knew. No leaks to the press." Dan shrugged, "One of his neighbors, somebody at work." He continued. "He took cash out on all three of his cards on 8th Avenue. Maximum so he's set for a while."

"Port Authority?"

"No sign of him. They only get thousands of people a day passing through the station. He's not someone who stands out."

"He's not a professional."

"No, but he's not dumb."

"Now, what?"

Dan didn't say, "I was hoping you'd have an idea." But "we're checking all transport out of the city, airports, train, bus. Even the YMCA's and low end hotels. The police haven't exactly been stopping everything to jump on it. When he runs out of money he'll resurface again."

"No chance he'll do it again?"

"I'd say no. But desperation throws a wrench into everything. I don't think he has a plan. He's a loner, no family, not many friends. He's not logging onto the Internet though he has more skills in that department than we do."

"So you're waiting."

Deke stayed behind as Cheryl left the office. "Not bad."

"I always wonder why she stays in this. She's got a nice family."

"It's in her blood, father, brother, they're all cops."

"Would you want your daughter to be a cop?"

"Hell no. I don't want to lose any more sleep than I already do."

***

Dan dug his heel into the mattress. He was sliding down a ravine. He woke with a start, shouting, as he was being pushed. When he got out of bed, he felt his knee pop and his head was heavy and ached though he only had one drink last night.

Spring was coming and soon the city would be full of kites and teenagers out drinking in the parks. Maggie would be back; he hadn't realized how much he missed her. She was the anchor to his life. Besides, he couldn't wait to unload Winnie who gave his days a routine he suspected was good for him but was leaving her tooth marks on all his furniture and barking all day long.

And then he needed to call Jess too. He glanced at the alarm clock, but it was way too early to call anyone. This was the hour for death calls. His mother died at dawn; Maggie had called him with the news. He shivered as he remembered. That thought led him to the inevitable other one.

Miranda. Dan repeated, "It wasn't my fault." She was drunk. She was always drunk by the end of whatever it was they were doing or wherever they ended up. Dan had been flirting but so what. Miranda always did as she pleased and got away with it while he paid the price for the most innocent of actions.

He'd never gotten over the guilt. And then the guilt for feeling relieved she was gone. No more, it echoed through his brain like a long sigh. No more fights, no more tears, no more picking up Miranda, drunk, off the floor. But there was no getting away from her, not really. "You win." He said to the empty kitchen.

He wasn't going to get out of this, the feeling of descending into a pit where the pain was sloshing around. Jess wasn't going to help him here. Sure, he liked her well enough but this was way beyond anything she could solve.

Dan took a long shower to see if he could clear his head. Miranda died in the spring, close to her birthday; she never made it to 37. That was supposed to be the year of straightening out, of making big changes in their lives. Miranda would stop drinking; they'd try again for a baby. She promised, but Dan took it with a grain of salt like every promise she had ever made. Anyway, back then, he was always busy with work, thinking about the future, of his job as detective where he was trying to prove himself. That's when it happened.

He let Maggie take over just like when his mother died. It took Dan two months off the job, and therapy, to be able to function enough to go back to work, but he never was the same again. The thick black clouds enveloped him, some days more than others, days like today where the pain was tangible.

He could light a candle. The little rituals were there to keep the darkness from taking over. Had she been trying to die for a long time? Was that what the drinking was all about? He would never really know if it was alcoholism or if there was something more to it all. Was Miranda trying to obliterate the conscious part of her to find a kind of peace in her life? And if so, why? What was it she wanted? Why hadn't he been able to help her?

She inhabited that same dark space where people from his work world dwelled. There were the junkies, the victims, the murderers. "Get a grip." Dan told himself. Miranda was not like them; Miranda was beautiful. The hot water in the shower was turning his skin bright pink. Purification rituals and punishing the flesh were the roots of his Catholicism. He dried himself off with more vigor than usual, further castigating his body.

Coffee, then his antacids. He toasted some frozen waffles from when he was eating better and ate four of them, three more than his diet allowed but at least his stomach felt good and warm inside for a change.

The phone rang. A man's body was found on Tupper Street in an alleyway. Sliced up. Deke was already there on the scene. The forensic team had secured the site and were bagging the evidence, cordoning off the alley and part of the street.

"Died last night." Deke said. Dan walked around the site to make sure they'd missed nothing. There was blood all over the sidewalk; knife wounds were messy. The man had white hair, a sweet smell emanated from his body, a mix of blood and alcohol.

"Another lost soul." Dan muttered to himself. "Check the shelters, the kitchens. No ID on the body."

"Like Santa Claus." Deke said, "Just missing the long white beard."

"It's the same guy. The one from the warehouse." Dan shivered in the damp cold air as he recognized the face. "Damn. He almost made it through the winter. Let's find out who the hell he is."

"Are you sure it's him?" Deke peered more closely into his face. "How can you tell?"

Dan didn't answer but muttered to himself. "Probably had his ID stolen ages ago."

Behind the body there was the telltale cart with a garbage bag. Dan would have to sort through it but first he needed to talk to the shopkeepers and bartenders in the area. Under a parked van across the street he spotted the knife. He called Deke over and shook his head. "They actually missed this."

"That's why you're here."

They spent another thirty minutes checking the area. Half the time police work was just this, walking around, hoping to find something. Then, the knife. Jackpot. Making sure you didn't screw up, training your eyes to see what wasn't there at first, but slowly came coming into focus with each step. That was what his job consisted of, a slow process.

As an ambulance took the body away, Dan's eyes filled up with tears. "This is getting bad." He never used to cry and now just about anything was setting him off.

Dan went into the print shop on the left of the alleyway. The owner started right in complaining, "I was sick of this guy creeping around out there. Pissing back there, going through the trash. I told him a hundred times to get out of there."

Dan listened to the middle-aged man who didn't have an ounce of sympathy for the dead man. For him, this was no more than getting rid of a stray dog that got in the way. The man went on. "He came into the shop once. You know how long it took to get rid of that stink."

"You know he was killed right there under your nose."

"Well, that's it. I have nothing to do with it. I'm calling my lawyer."

Dan was shocked. This man could have easily gone the other way, helping the old man, giving him a cup of coffee, even calling the police to pick him up if it came to that. Anything would have been better. They could have taken him to the shelter again. It was a stupid, senseless crime.

***

"Coffee?" Deke looked at Dan as he headed towards the car.

"Ok." Though Dan knew he shouldn't.

***

At the end of the day Dan stopped at St. Louis Cathedral on Main Street and lit a candle. He took a seat in a pew and closed his eyes for a moment. Miranda. It was her birthday. April 19th.

"Dan," The priest, Father Jack Kazmerack touched his shoulder. "Everything all right?"

Dan nodded.

"Would you like a coffee?"

They walked back to the rectory where another door opened into Father's apartment. "It's too late for coffee. Let me get you a drink. Sherry, which I have for the ladies, or whiskey?"

Dan knew the priest had the good stuff. "Whiskey."

"A hard day?"

"Death day. Miranda's birthday. And it never fails, someone always gets killed right on schedule, like an anniversary in her honor."

"Of course. Miranda." He'd married them and smiled, remembering. "Ice?"

"No, thanks."

"I saw the news. An old man."

"Sad."

"You have that all the time."

"You do too." Dan wasn't sure what the priest was referring to but assumed it was the simple fact of death.

"In a simpler way. My parishioners are getting old. I lose about one a week on average now." Father Kazmerack paused. "You know what your problem is, Dan."

"Please, tell me. I'm all ears." Dan said with a bite of sarcasm.

"You don't believe in redemption."

"In my line of work?"

"Especially in your work. And stop torturing yourself. Pure egotism, you're not God. You didn't make Miranda die." His voice softened. "Now, she was special."

"That she was."

"I loved her too. With all her complications. We all did. But you know, it's been a long time."

"Eight years."

"It's not your fault. You need to believe that. You can be happy again; there's time if you let yourself."

"I wish you could do one of those slaps to my forehead like those TV evangelists. Heal, and it would all be gone. No more of this."

"Now that would be one way to do it. I could try. But then you'd lose the beauty of her, too. Wouldn't want that." Jack smiled at him. "Stay for dinner. We're having a nice goulash. Cook makes the real thing, she's from the old country."

When he got home, Dan checked his messages, Maggie and Jess. He debated which one to call first; most likely Maggie had remembered the date and was worried. The first few years after the fact, Dan got stinking drunk to commemorate the occasion. He never knew exactly how he got home. Sometimes it turned into a binge for a few days and then Deke would find him in one of the old downtown bars and straighten him out and get him back to work just in time before his job was in danger.

Miranda's birthday had always been a big event during their marriage; she expected no less. There were big expensive presents and special dinners out, washed down with abundant wine. One year he cooked lobsters and presented her with a diamond pendant that blazed light. Internal and external light he thought watching her lying on the bed after he'd taken off her black stockings, one at a time. On special occasions she'd wear a black lace garter though she complained Dan found it too appealing. "It's the stockings, not me that you want." But still, she indulged him. Then she was naked except for the necklace.

***

It was almost eleven but he called Jess. "I hope it's not too late. I had another case today."

"Is it always like this?"

"Maybe. When can I see you?"

"The weekend."

"Junior around?"

"No. How about a little more antiquing?"

"Please."

"You choose then."

"Really? Well, let me see what fun activity I can come up with."

"I'm glad you called."

"It's good to talk to you too."

***

After he hung up, he could no longer control the memory. It happened on the 25th anniversary party for a workmate of Miranda's, Liz and her husband, Steve. The house was decorated with silver balloons and streamers. Dan's first thought when he walked in the door was that he and Miranda would never make it that long; twenty-five years was an entire lifetime and the drama that their lives had turned into wasn't made for the long run.

Dan was relieved to see no clergy in sight; no sign the couple were going to be repeating their vows. He couldn't handle any romance. It was an ordinary happy event. Champagne and mixed drinks were being served at a bar set up in the corner of the living room; Miranda made a beeline for it as soon as they got in the door. "No sense wasting time." Dan thought as he kept an eye on her.

Dan watched her holding a glass of champagne, toasting the couple with a wide smile. Then she moved through the room like she was floating; her long blond hair was loose; she was in a low cut dark green dress with tiny straps. Dan thought of the many times he watched her this way. Probably half the men in the room were watching her; she was that beautiful. That's what surprised Dan, that after all the drunken scenes she could still be so alluring, so graceful and light, an angel floating through air.

Since Dan made detective, he'd been sticking to his three drink limit. He couldn't afford to be hungover if a call came in and one could at any hour. But he started directly on a vodka martini, clear and pure, he liked to think. The bartender had a heavy hand. It burned going down but then offered Dan a glimpse of freedom, a way out of all his thoughts.

The highlight of the party was a buffet with lobsters staring from their red posts with their beady eyes. Dan tried to see if Miranda might actually be eating something; she loved seafood, but the table was too crowded to approach. Buffets brought out the greed in people. Dan hated them; people lined up and acted as if they'd never eaten in their lives.

He caught up with her in the kitchen where she was eating a plain cracker. He touched her shoulder. "Hey, Miranda."

"What's up?" Her voice bore the slightest trace of annoyance.

"Did you try the shrimp?"

"Delish." She answered turning back to her conversation with a couple of teachers from her school.

"Would you join me?"

"Later, not now Dan." She glared at him. Miranda believed a party was for going off on her own. They saw each other every day, no reason to stick to each other like glue when they were out.

"Go ahead, Dan." Liz said. "We'll catch up with you."

Dan knew that meant Liz would be watching out for Miranda even though it was her big day. Dan appreciated the kindness so he went back to the living room and sat with Gail, another one of the teachers he'd met before at a school function. They finished eating and Dan went for a second martini. The party was getting louder and darker as if his vision was becoming a tunnel of light against a backdrop of black.

Someone had cleared the furniture in the family room and turned up the music. Rhythm and blues from the sixties was followed by an old disco mix. "You're too young for that." He said to Gail.

"I love it."

"Really?"

"Even the disco. Everyone thinks I'm crazy."

"Do you want to dance?" Though it wasn't Dan's favorite activity, the martini, spurred him on. At that point he didn't care how foolish he looked.

Miranda flew by him. "What the hell are you doing?" Her voice raged. Dan reached for her arm to calm her down. "Fuck you. Don't you dare touch me." She shouted at him and then a moment later, she was gone.

Gail abruptly stopped dancing. "What was that all about? She was so happy before and so pretty. I'm sorry."

"I should go get her." Dan could hardly bring himself to move. He downed the rest of his drink and went to look for her. He stopped Liz, "Where's Miranda?"

"I don't know. I don't see her in here. Try the kitchen. She was hanging out with the girls."

Dan looked around the house and was waylaid by Steve, offering him another drink. Though he didn't want it, he took it in his hand. When he walked outside he didn't see the car anywhere. "Shit, she took the car." He usually kept the keys away from her but Miranda must have brought her own set. More than once he'd stopped her from driving but usually she knew better than to touch his car. "What the hell is wrong with you?" He said it to no one. But she had driven drunk before, probably more times than he ever suspected and somehow managed to get home.

Gail followed him out. "I'll give you a ride. I didn't mean anything. We were just dancing."

"It's not you. Miranda has a drinking problem." He was just straight enough to realize how ridiculous it sounded coming from a guy half in the bag himself.

There was no car in the driveway when he got home. The pit of his stomach was hollow. He called Deke to warn him Miranda was out driving. Dan stayed up all night, drinking coffee, trying to quell the fear that wouldn't go away.

At six in the morning they found her on the thruway to Albany, smashed into a guardrail. Albany, where the hell was she going?" It was the question he'd asked a thousand times. "Why Albany?" There was no answer. Miranda could have just started out driving on the straightest and fastest road she could find.

The rest of the day was a blur with Maggie and Miranda's father waiting with Dan in the house. Deke took care of the arrangements to bring her back to Buffalo and from that point on Maggie took over.

 No one said a word but Dan knew he had fucked up. His job was to protect Miranda and take care of her.

Maggie sat with him across the kitchen table. "She had a problem. Everyone knew that. It was just a question of time until something happened to her."

"I should have gone after her. She wanted me to."

"You don't know that. You couldn't watch her every minute."

Dan relived that night a thousand times. Each time he went after her and apologized practically down on his knees. He brought her home and they made love like they had once upon a time.

The funeral was a rain-soaked blur. After the mass, everyone met back at Dan's house. Dan started throwing back shots at eleven in the morning, until he could talk to the people who came. Even the house seemed foreign to him, like he was seeing it for the first time and not recognizing it. And it was the first time, the first time without Miranda in it.

Maggie managed all the details, even saying goodbye to the first graders who made a big poster with all their messages to Miranda. Dan added it to the boxes of her belongings. He went from the bathroom and bedroom filling boxes with her things without stopping to look at them. Then he took them down to the basement, not able to look at anything until a few years had passed. After the funeral, Dan made it a point not to see any of Miranda's friends. Every once in a while he'd run into Liz at the supermarket. Both were quiet, still numb, but Liz always gave him a hug.

Dan read the police report and the insurance report a million times. Inconclusive skid marks in the snow. She was speeding and lost control. Was that all? He would pronounce her name out loud sometimes when he was alone; Miranda, a flamboyant name, a big name for a big person with flair and character. It had been one of the many things he loved about her.

Her death defined him. If once he had been quick in all his movements and slightly angry and impatient, afterwards he was slower, his head bowed. Those first months when Dan got back to work, he took risks, the first to answer a call, to approach a robber or even a gunman. Deke finally said to him, "Cut it out. It ain't going to do you any good to die too."

Chapter Eight

Dan felt his heart beat a little faster as soon as he saw Jess's car pull up. Dan opened the door for her and gave her a hug. He was doing the driving out to Warsaw, a small town in Wyoming County, southeast of Buffalo. They were driving out to check out the maple syrup tapping and to get out of the city. Jess was in a down jacket and wool hat which she shed in his car. "Don't go any further." Dan smiled at her. "I've missed you."

"How cold is it going to be?"

"You look ready for an expedition to the north pole."

"I need mittens. I only have gloves."

"I bet Chris doesn't even own a pair of mittens."

"They grow up too fast. They never have mittens. I miss when she was little."

"She'll be ok."

"I hope so. You've been working a lot."

"It depends on who's knifing who these days."

"Or that little boy still."

"We're stuck."

"Oh." Jess didn't say anymore.

"Maggie is making dinner tonight."

Jess looked at him raising an eyebrow, "Meeting your family?"

"Well, just Maggie. Todd probably won't come."

"Okay."

Dan had an old school friend who lived out this way, in a house just up the hill just before the entrance into town. Joey was waiting for them. He was divorced now, but some years ago they had made a foursome with their wives.

Joey looked older, his stomach over his jeans, with dark circles under his eyes more pronounced than Dan remembered. "Joseph, my man." Dan hugged him. "Too long."

The house was a spectacular Victorian with huge rooms and original woodwork. The kids lived in Rochester with their mom so Joey had all this space to himself.

"You look a bit green around the gills." Dan commented.

"Small town life." Joey smiled. "I was out with the boys last night. "Come on, Jess, let me show you my pride and joy."

Dan stayed in the kitchen while they toured the house. Today, the big empty house made him sad. If Miranda were still alive, would he be alone or would they be visiting Joey?"

"It's gorgeous." Jess said, "It would be my dream to have a farmhouse with five bedrooms."

"Are you sure you'd want to live in a small town?"

"Close enough. I'd like to be in the country in a farmhouse."

"With animals?"

"Dozens. Chickens, goats, even cows."

"I can picture the house, but not you slopping the pigs." Dan commented.

"My grandparents had a dairy farm in Michigan. I spent a lot of summers there."

Joey interrupted them and gave them his best BBC butler voice. "Lunch will be served shortly in the dining room."

"You didn't have to do that." Dan protested. "We could have taken you out."

"No problem. I know you won't believe it but my cooking has improved."

"Gone domestic. God help us."

Jess stood up but Joey motioned her to sit. "No, you relax. Dan said you had a very busy tax season. What would you like to drink? Put on some music."

Dan opened beers, took one to Jess, and then went back into the kitchen to keep Joey company. "Is everything okay?"

"Not bad. Sorry about the hangover. I don't usually drink like that but it was a stag; I had to go."

"They still do those. Good God." Dan remembered his own, a drinking marathon with Joey present. It had been innocent enough, just dinner and four or five bars with the booze flowing.

"That's what I say."

"I haven't been to one in more than ten years."

"You're getting old my boy."

"How's work?"

Joey worked for the county analyzing water and soil. "It's not bad. How about you? Saw your boss on television a couple of times. The case of that little boy. Any news?"

"Not much. I should be looking around for another job if I don't find something soon."

"You always say that."

"Are you seeing anyone?"

"Dan, you're like an old lady. Like my mother."

"So, no, I guess."

Joey laughed. "It looks like you got lucky."

"That's right."

***

"Too many meals. I'm sorry about that." Dan said when they got into the car.

"I can always eat." Jess responded.

"Bad planning on my part."

"It's fine. I'm enjoying it." Dan was driving just past the speed limit so they wouldn't be late for Maggie's. "Watch out or you'll get a ticket." Jess said.

"No, I know the speed traps. I haven't even digested lunch yet." Dan wasn't sure if the afternoon in the country was a success. Joey had made a huge roast beef lunch but the atmosphere was off. Joey was tired and instead of his usual fun self, he gave the impression of a lonely man stuck in the middle of nowhere. Dan stopped to pick up some wine at Premier Liquor. A couple of beers at Joey's and now wine with his sister." Too much alcohol?" He asked Jess.

"No. It's the weekend. My big season is over. I can celebrate. Plus it makes me horny so I don't think you'll object."

"Are you sure it's not the maple trees? All that sap running?" In fact, they never got to see more than the trees in the distance and pictures of tapping them in the shop where they bought syrup.

***

Maggie was waiting for them with the dining room table set. "I hope you didn't work too hard." Dan kissed her.

"No, the miracles of the supermarket. I was on call today." Maggie turned to Jess. "You're Jess." She held out her hand. "Come on in."

"How was Florida?"

"Fantastic. The beach was pure white sand. I saw dolphins, pelicans and did nothing more strenuous than choose which restaurant to go for dinner."

"You look wonderful." Maggie was tanned, her hair showing some blond streaks. She even looked younger. "Guess who we saw today." Dan asked as he handed her a bottle of wine and a jug of maple syrup.

"Not a clue." Maggie poured them wine from a bottle she had breathing on the counter.

"Joey."

"No kidding. Joey. You should have invited him. God, Joey. That explains this." She looked at the syrup. "Very nice. See, it doesn't have to come from Vermont."

"Joey's still in Warsaw."

"How long has it been?"

"Fifteen years living there. I usually see him once a year or so and he comes up for conferences."

"Is he still cute?"

"He's cute." Jess answered.

"God, he was a pain in the ass." Maggie went on.

"When you were ten and we were six. He had a crush on you for years."

They got through two bottles of wine. Dan felt exhausted. Leaving Maggie's he told her. "I wish we'd spent the day together. I'm sorry. We don't have much time and we spent the whole day with other people."

"No, it was great meeting them." She invited him in.

"I'm too tired. I'm sorry." It was one in the morning.

"You can just sleep you know."

"I've heard that before." But he followed Jess into the house.

Dan was determined to make it work. She was sitting on the sofa and they kissed for what seemed like an eternity. Then Dan lifted up her sweater. "Are you cold?" She shivered as he rubbed her nipples between his fingers, first one and then the other. "Do you feel that?"

She nodded and he continued until she was rubbing against him. "Wait," he said returning to kissing her. Then he put his mouth on her neck, moving down to the breasts and taking them into his mouth. Then he asked, "Do you feel that? In your cunt?"

Jess nodded. Only then did he begin to touch her first over her jeans, rubbing his hand in a circular motion.

She unzipped her jeans and tried to wriggle out of them. "Slowly." He said and kissed her again. She put a hand on his penis in an attempt to speed things up but as he put his hand inside her panties, working on a rhythm.

"Harder," she said. He pressed on until she came. He tried to keep up the stimulus but he had been hard so long he exploded almost as soon as he entered her. Dan was recovering his breath, his heart pounding in his chest. It would do for now. When he was dating a few years ago, he sometimes found women who were like that, the connection from brain to sex severed. Maggie had enlightened him by quoting abuse statistics. "How do you expect them to respond?" It made Dan wonder how they ever managed to get over it.

He didn't think that was Jess's case; she was at ease with her body. How long would it take? Maybe it would never work. Maybe it was just chemistry not working. He pulled her next to him, her body fit his well and was so lovely. It was a shame.

***

"You're not what I thought you'd be." Jess picked up her cup of coffee and took a sip, in an effort to shake off sleep.

"No?" Dan looked up from the paper, his curiosity aroused. "How so?"

"More layers to you. You're a deeper person."

"So, is that good or bad?"

"Good. You think about everything. I can see the wheels turning up there." She pointed to her temple.

"Only practical things. I'm no intellectual."

"You do all right. Plus you're cute."

"Two compliments. I must have been really good last night."

"Or I was."

"You were."

"For a cop, you're not all that macho."

"Darn. That's what I'm aiming for."

"You look like you would be. I was a little afraid to go out with you."

"Really?" This would have been the moment to talk future with Jess, but Dan just couldn't bring himself to do so instead he changed the topic completely. "Can I ask you a weird question? Can you see her around me?" Dan asked. He didn't need to say more.

"Sometimes."

"How can I get that to stop?"

"Cut the ties with her, let her go."

Dan had a flash of being cut off from his source, his own vitality. Maybe he'd lose all his ability to feel anything at all. "How does one do that?" He had his formal detective tone to his voice.

"Talk to her, let her go. Tell her you loved her, that you're sorry."

Dan let that slide though he'd never told Jess any details about Miranda's death. "Is all this normal?"

"For me. But then, I'm spooky lady, remember." Then she laughed when she saw his expression, "Sure it is."

"Is it a problem for you?"

"We're not having chats in bed or anything. Do you feel her around?"

"I never thought about it. Maybe I do, but it's been a long time since she died."

"You need to talk to a therapist."

"I did all that."

"Burn a candle. Go to church."

"I do every year on her birthday. I don't want to forget her. I just want to be able to handle it better."

"Just because she's dead doesn't mean you can't make peace with her."

***

There was a report on his desk. Petey's clothes had stains that could have been from an emollient. Skin cream just as

Dan as suspected. Flakes of skin that were not his. A match on the rug in the apartment.

Dan got on the phone. "Edgar, you did it!"

"Do you know how many beige carpets there are in the city of Buffalo?"

"Hey, as long as it's the one in Clark's digs, we are set."

Dan smiled. Today was the day! New bank information was lying on his desk too. Florida, not a bad place to be in early spring. Daytona, then Miami, Clark had hit the road. That guy was frugal enough, his cash was lasting longer than they'd expected. Dan considered flying down. For one thing, he was starting to get a sense of Aaron Clark, and he cared a lot more about finding him than an overworked Dade county cop would.

He looked at the address of the ATM. If he got moving, he could make it by late afternoon. He got on the phone with Dario, a guy from the Miami police department he met a couple of years ago on a case. "We need to pick this guy up." Dan filled him in. "This might be the closest we get to him. Check out the cheap motels, anything around the bus station."

"Dan, I know my job."

"Sorry. We've been on this for quite a while. Everyone is getting restless." Dan said, "I could come down."

"What for? You don't know the city. It'll take you too long. We're on it. Relax. Didn't we get you the bank info?"

What would this guy be doing in Miami? Getting some sun before he gave himself up? Maybe there was a friend he had down there but for a loner like Clark that wasn't very likely.

An hour later, Dario called back. "He's on his way to Charlotte Amalie. The same credit card number with the name, Steven Jenkins."

"Where the hell is that?"

"St. Thomas. Virgin Islands, the U.S."

"What would he be doing there?"

"Maybe he likes fishing. Two million tourists a year. A place to chill."

"Wouldn't he stick out with those cruise tourists? How much time have we got?"

***

He and Deke could get a flight out of New York and get there to meet the guy's plane. He punched Cheryl's number. "He's on his way to the airport to Charlotte Amalie."

"Why?"

"Can't answer that. We can be at the airport in Miami before he shows up for the flight."

"How do you know he'll be on it? He hasn't shown any signs of being that stupid yet."

Deke came into his office holding a pair of handcuffs. "It's been awhile since I used these."

"Let's hope we get to."

Jet Blue airlines took them to New York, then they got a direct flight to Miami. They'd be getting in at three if there were no delays. Dan felt the excitement rise. This was it. Deke sat in his seat playing video games on the New York leg.

"You don't play enough of those with your kids?"

"I'm preparing. Got to beat them some time."

They rushed through the air train to make their flight. "It'll be warm there." Deke said. "Didn't even have time to check the weather."

"It won't be hot, just the low 80's. Dan took off his jacket. "The tourists must all show up like us, in snowsuits." Dan wished he'd left his overcoat in his car. Now he'd be carrying it with him all day. "I always wanted to go somewhere warm in the middle of winter. Not this way, but you know what I mean."

Deke said, "Sure, with Jess, the beach. Sun. What's that drink, sex on the beach?"

"The sex could be better."

"You're kidding. She looks..." Deke didn't finish.

"It's complicated." Dan didn't know why he was saying this to Deke or to anyone at all.

"Maybe with time, it'll get better."

"Do you think some couples just don't work together?"

"Never thought about it."

"It's not that it's bad. Let's face it, how bad can it be. It's just not exciting."

Deke grunted. "You're not a teenager."

"No, but I'm not a pensioner either."

"Well, you like her."

"Yes." Dan picked up his file complete with pictures, including the fuzzy ones off the bank cameras. Dan wanted to make sure they wouldn't miss him. Ideally they'd pick him up as he showed up for his flight. All they needed was a bit of luck, no delays and the police ready for action.

"Ten minutes." Dan shifted in his seat.

"Shit, what'd they say?" Deke opened his eyes.

"Third in line for takeoff. JFK is always like this."

Dan felt the dampness under his arms. One thing he liked about Deke was he never looked nervous.

***

Deke looked over at his friend. Dan had been his idea of superman, back when they were in their 20's. He was the fastest and smartest cop of their class. Then Miranda came into his life and now, complications with Jess. But Dan was sure unlucky with women. "Hey Dan."

"Yeah."

"It's supposed to be fun. Don't work too hard with Jess. If it doesn't work, it doesn't work."

"Let's see if we ever get off the ground here."

"Relax."

***

When they landed, Dan called Dario. They planned to meet by check in for United and then head up to the gate.

Deke looked around and said. "You'd never know we were in Miami. All airports look the same these days."

"The light is different, and there are palm trees." Dan willed himself to take a deep breath and relax. "There's sun too, for a change." He checked his watch. They had an hour. Dan took off his jacket and was carrying it along with his overcoat.

He shook hands with Dario.

"It doesn't look good."

"What?"

"They're closing the gate in a few minutes. No sign of the guy." The three of them sat in the waiting area.

"How long should we give it?" Deke asked.

"A set up." Dan said. He went to talk to the woman at the counter. There were three passengers who didn't check in. Clark was one of them. She was closing down. "He has officially missed the flight?"

"But with an e-ticket could we have missed him somehow?"

"We'd have a record."

Dan went up with her just to make sure. He walked through the plane once. It was a small commuter jet so there were less than fifty people on board and plenty of empty seats. He went back downstairs. Deke was on his phone. Dario was tapping his foot.

"We'll give it another hour just in case."

"Well, he's smart enough to get another ID." Deke said.

"Yeah, but not a credit card."

***

Aaron Clark wanted to see just who was after him so he watched from behind a post near a coffee shop. He wanted to know how much manpower they were putting into his case and how important he was. The plan set him back two hundred dollars but he had to know. He spotted the three men almost immediately. The Buffalo guys were in suits carrying coats and the one from Miami was in a short sleeved shirt. That was a bad sign. "Undercover, yeah, right." Aaron felt better seeing how incompetent they could be but still worried they'd made such a big effort to pick him up. He walked out of the terminal and took the bus back into the city.

***

"So we call it quits?" Deke looked up. It was 6.

"Get a flight back."

"What's your hurry? Let's get some dinner. You don't want to head back to Buffalo just yet. Come on. It's my treat." Dario smiled. "Little Havana. Dan, you remember, don't you?" They worked together on a drug murder two years ago and had struck up a friendship. Dario had been going through a divorce and after work, they drowned their sorrows in a large number of Cuba libres.

The temperature was a balmy 80."Hey, feel that sun. I haven't felt that in months." Deke said.

"A tropical interlude, thanks to the department." Dan commented.

"No, thanks to Aaron Clark. He could have picked a lot worse."

Dan booked the last flight at ten. If there weren't too many delays, they'd make it back to Buffalo by midnight.

Chapter Nine

"So what the hell was that all about?" Cheryl had Deke and Dan in her office the next morning. "Taxpayers will enjoy paying for that little excursion. So where is he?"

Dan's shoulders slumped. "Don't know." All those hours for nothing, on the plane trip back, neither he nor Deke had said a word.

Clarisse stopped by Dan's office later. "Heard you had a little tropical vacation. So where's the suntan?" Dan knew he was in for it from the rest of the department.

Maggie called. "Dinner tonight?"

"I'm really beat."

"Come on. You've got to eat. Just drag your body over."

"Is eight too late? I've got to check on something first."

Dan drove over to the West Side. A Mrs. Carson died in her apartment, gassed apparently. The windows were wide open and the wind was blowing papers around. "Great," Dan thought. "There goes any evidence." The fire department had done the obvious by opening the windows to air out the place. The apartment wasn't just cold, it was freezing.

86, she'd died in the bedroom. She lived alone; the house told her story as he walked around the rooms. A path of dirt was etched into the linoleum when her failing eyesight probably could no longer see how dirty it was. Dishes were piled high in the kitchen and piles of clothes were all over the living room and bedroom. She probably couldn't keep up with simple chores.

"She put the oven on to maybe to get a little more heat into the place, and fell asleep. She's lucky the place didn't blow." Clarisse told him. She'd beaten him to the scene.

"Looks pretty clear cut."

"Sad way to go."

"Easy, painless. I'd say it's a sad way to live."

***

Dan hugged Maggie. "Come in." She took his coat. "See it was a good idea."

"You didn't go to any trouble I hope."

"No, you know me. When I've got time I cook, I like to." She handed him a glass of wine. "You look like you could use it."

"How did you know?"

"Sixth sense. I won't even ask about work. How's the romance going?"

"It's going."

"She's really beautiful."

"You want to say, what's she doing with me?"

"No, silly. Just an innocent observation. You always want your partners to be beautiful, don't you. Remind you of anyone?"

"She's nothing like Miranda."

"I hope not." Maggie shook her head. "Sorry, I didn't mean that. I meant like Miranda, she's attractive. You know what I mean."

"Sure. Sure." He smiled, liking to see Maggie in a tough spot. "Nothing in that case is working out right. Now, I'm really looking like an ass."

Maggie got it out of him. She always did and Dan ended up telling her about the trip. "He'll slip up. You've just got to be patient."

"He's smarter than I thought. So enough of that. What's new with you?"

"I met someone."

"No kidding."

"Katie's neighbor. I've known her for years and I was over there for dinner and he came over , and we got to talking and hit it off."

Dan listened to all the details. If anyone deserved to be happy it was Maggie and maybe that meant a having relationship. He just wondered why humans couldn't be happy alone.

***

When he got home he called Jess. "Hey, how are you?"

"She was caught shoplifting. I guess it's the typical kid thing but I'll tell you, I am furious."

"Chris?"

"Who else?" Jess's tone was impatient.

"She's too young. They won't do anything."

"Craig just lost it. He wants to send her to a boarding school in Vermont. Can you believe it? He won't even let her finish out the year here."

"Don't you have a say in that? Call your lawyer."

"I keep hoping he'll listen to me."

"Has he before?'

"He's her father. He should care about what happens to her."

"Let me know if there's anything I can do."

"You could come over."

"It's late. Don't you have to get up early?"

"That doesn't matter."

Dan got into his car and headed over though he was more tired than he could remember, after the trip and realizing just how stupid he had been.

Jess opened the door. "Thanks for coming."

"No problem." He sat next to her on the sofa, fighting sleep.

"You really look beat."

"I was on a plane last night."

"I didn't know or I wouldn't have asked you. Let's go to bed then." Dan fell asleep the moment he stretched out.

Jess was already dressed in the kitchen having breakfast when he woke up and made his way downstairs. "You didn't wake me up."

"You're fine. It's only 7:00. Coffee?" She poured him a cup.

"Thanks. I wasn't much help." He'd had the foresight to change his clothes before he came over so he could go directly to work.

"I'm going to drive over and take Chris to school but stay as long as you need. There's cereal and toast. Soak up some of that acid you love so much."

Dan had another cup of coffee and then, because he had never been alone in her house, he looked around. He wondered why there were no antiques in the house since she liked them so much. In the kitchen Jess had nice shiny pots and pans, probably a set she got as a wedding gift. She didn't use any of them or the food processor that sat on the counter. There was a shelf jammed with cookbooks that confirmed his theory that the less you cooked the more stuff related to cooking you accumulated. Her taste in cookbooks leaned towards complicated chocolate desserts and Indian cuisine.

The first time he stayed over, the only place he looked was the medicine cabinet and found nothing interesting. He wasn't really suspicious of Jess or even looking for anything specific. He didn't want to be surprised to find out the woman he was dating was hooked on Vicodin or something worse.

The only thing he found was a vibrator in the drawer under the kitchen sink which made him smile. Kinky for the kitchen or she maybe just supposed Chris wouldn't look there. He was also relieved; at least she was interested enough in sex to have one.

Dan hadn't brought a razor with him and looked around the bathroom for one of hers. He found a pink Bic and strawberry scented shaving cream. He scraped away at his cheeks. He looked like hell; his dark circles reached down to his cheekbones. Even after shaving he had a 5 o'clock shadow. He tossed the razor into the trash and spotted something that looked very familiar to him. He reached in and pulled out a pregnancy test stick. "Jesus Christ." His heart beat faster like it was rising in his chest. No line. No color change. "Thank God." He exhaled. "So when were you going to tell me about this?" He said out loud.

***

The autopsy report for Mrs. Carson sat on his desk. She was dead before she was gassed. Dan looked at the report a second time. There were no unusual marks on her body, nothing that suggested anything other than a peaceful natural death. Damn. Suicide? There was a cocktail in her blood of sleeping pills, Lipitor, and some Tylenol to top it off and something Dan had never heard of, kava kava. The little mix had caused liver failure. He got on the phone to Deke. Then, he'd start calling on the neighbors.

"Bad news." He said to Clarisse as she came into the office. After Deke, Clarisse was his favorite person in the department. She was as tall as he was, overweight, but she carried it nicely. She was strong and took no shit but could be soft when the situation required it, like giving bad news which was why she got stuck doing it so often.

"The Johnson boy?" She asked.

"No. The woman who was gassed. Well, her blood was full of all kinds of drugs- prescription and not."

"Suicide?"

"Possibly. We've got to make sure."

"Let's hope so. If not, this is turning into murder capital, USA."

"So how're the kids?"

"Did I tell you. Kecia's on the honor roll. Teddy is playing basketball."

"He any good?"

"It doesn't matter; it's discipline." She shrugged.

"With you as their mom, that's not going to be a problem."

"Heard you got yourself a girl."

"Gossipmongers, all of you."

"Gorgeous, I hear."

"Next I'll hear I'm dating a top model.'

"No. I know you. You don't like them that thin."

***

Mrs. Carson had a daughter in Pittsburgh and a son in Lockport. They would be at the funeral. Deke reported to Dan. "The daughter has bad arthritis. She doesn't get up here much to see her mother."

"What about the son?"

"He saw her once a month, brought over 500 bucks to give her a hand."

"You wouldn't know it from the way she was living. What was her pension like?"

"Not much more than a thousand. Her husband died young. She worked in a shoe store but she owned her house."

"She could have had someone come and help or got one of those programs like meals on wheels."

"Sometimes these old people get stubborn. Her son said she was afraid they'd put her in a home."

"You'd think having kids would spare you that."

"Thanks, Dan." Deke smiled at him.

"So she took a mess of pills, whatever she had lying around, then turned on the gas for good measure. We'll have to see if she was sick."

"At that age they're all sick."

"I mean something serious."

"Nothing strong in her medicine chest." Deke said. "Maybe she got tired of life. What did you find out about the neighbors?"

"One is about 80 himself but in pretty good shape; he practices natural medicine, a quack I'd say. He did the shopping for her."

"I'm going to call him. One of the substances in her blood one of those health food store products. Kava Kava. Ever hear of it?" Dan googled it and found out it was used to reduce stress, as a kind of relaxant and its sales were banned in Europe. It was originally used in the Pacific as a drink like alcohol was here, to get high.

Deke shook his head. "No controls on any of the crap out there. And I want them to stop selling that shit online."

"I'm going to talk to that neighbor."

"What for? She's old; she died. You don't have enough problems? Case closed."

Dan shook his head. "You want to end up like that?"

***

"Mr. Owens," Dan led the older man into the office. "Come in. Sit down. I'd like to talk to you about Mrs. Carson."

He was older but agile. Spry was the word that came to Dan's mind. "Okay.'

"What was your relationship with your neighbor?"

"Just that. She was my neighbor."

"Did you recommend she take any vitamins or supplements?"

"We talked. She was alone so I checked up on her every couple of days; sometimes I did some shopping for her. She was afraid to drive so it was hard for her to get to the supermarket. I might have recommended some B vitamins or something for stress. Mostly I told her she had to get out and get some exercise."

"Kava kava?"

"Possibly. I don't remember. Why?"

"It was in her blood along with painkillers. Was she depressed?"

"Yes. She was terrified they'd take her home away from her. That was all she thought about."

Dan felt sorry for the old woman. "You're not a doctor. You can't go around recommending or prescribing. You can be prosecuted for that."

"That's not what I do. I'm licensed as a naturopath in France; I spent some years there. If I hadn't checked in on Rita, she would have been totally alone."

"Well, this is America. We don't recognize natural medicine."

"That's because you've got such a great health care system, right?"

***

When Jess called, Dan wasn't sure what to say but she immediately started talking about Chris. "She's scared and being super nice and obedient."

"She's not a bad kid. This might set her straight on things." Dan was relieved not to mention his discovery. He wasn't ready yet.

"Craig is not giving an inch. He wants her in that school next month."

"Don't let him do it. Get a lawyer. Get a new agreement and take Jess. Stop him."

"I don't know if I can."

"Be firm. How do you know he doesn't want a little freedom from fatherhood and this is his easy way out, to ship her off?" He finished his pep talk for Jess. He could have used one too. Nothing was clear cut these days, not even the death of an 85-year-old woman. Why couldn't she just have gone in her sleep?

"When can I see you, Dan?"

"I'm really busy now. Let me give you a call."

"Anything wrong?"

"No. The usual, you know, cases with no solutions."

By the third phone call of the week, Jess was getting frustrated. "What's up? Are you avoiding me?"

"No, no. I'm so busy."

"It's not because of Chris, is it?"

"Of course not." Dan was surprised she would think so.

"Well, it's a hard situation and I've been really stressed about it."

"I'm sorry. It's not Chris."

"Well, then."

"Okay." Dan took a deep breath. "The last time I was at your house I had to borrow your razor and as I was throwing it out I saw…"

"Don't tell me you're rooting through my trash. I can't believe it."

"Not rooting. I saw it and recognized it. My wife was trying to get pregnant for years."

"So."

"Well, tell me then. Are you trying to get pregnant?"

"No, just a scare. Nothing major. It happens."

"It shouldn't."

"What about your part in that or are we talking about virgin birth?"

"I thought we talked about birth control, the first times I used a condom, and then you said you had an IUD which I assumed was working."

"I had it removed."

"Without saying anything to me."

"I was using a cap."

"Jess, I don't want children. Really I don't. And if this happened." He didn't finish the sentence.

"What? Is that a threat?"

"Of course not. I'm sorry it happened."

"Do you think I want a child? Don't you think I have enough with Chris?"

"I want to make sure. I don't want any surprises. Do you know that half of all pregnancies are unplanned?"

"Well, let's say then some men had better get on the case and be more responsible."

"Some men, meaning me. Listen, I've got to get back to work. I'll call you in a couple of days and we can talk."

***

Deke came into Dan's office. "It's that time of year again. Old Rob's birthday."

"I completely forgot. What are you getting him?"

"Patti does that." Patti was his wife.

"I never know what to get."

"Call Sylvia and ask."

"Good idea. Hope I get her. Rob usually picks up."

Dan punched the number in and was lucky. "How is he?"

Sylvia answered, "He has some good days. The medication keeps the shaking down. He's excited about seeing you guys."

"That's why I'm calling. What should I bring?"

"Dan, you don't have to bring anything."

"I want to."

"A book. He's reading history now."

"Good. That crime fiction stint was doing a number on his brain."

***

Dan popped over to the bookstore downtown which was more deserted than ever after all the shops moved out to the suburbs. It broke his heart. He remembered his mother taking him and Maggie downtown back in the days when there were several department stores and the bustle of a real city. They always stopped for pizza afterwards. Sometimes they went to the movies.

Dan found a biography of Ben Franklin that looked appealing. It had been ages since he'd picked up a book. He gravitated towards the new age section and found a book on Lily Dale written by a regular press journalist, not some new age writer. "All right." He was looking forward to finding out more about that strange world of spirits.

***

Sylvia answered the door in a dark purple dress. With makeup and jewelry she looked younger than her 60 years. Dan wished he'd put on a nicer shirt but there hadn't been any time after work to go home and change. She kissed Dan on the cheek and led him into the living room. Rob was sitting in an armchair with pillows propped up behind his back. "You won't mind if I don't get up."

Dan shook his hand. Rob had to take an early retirement at 55 when the Parkinson's started to interfere with his work. That's when Cheryl came into the picture and took over the department. "You're looking well."

"Could be worse."

Dan wondered where Deke was. Dan had never been close to Rob like Deke was. There had been too many conflicts because Rob ran the show in the old school way, strictly with no shades of gray, his way or no way at all. Friendship had been imposed by the rigors of work and the need to chill out afterwards over drinks at the nearest bar. Rob had even warned him about Miranda. Back then it made Dan annoyed, like Rob was over-stepping some invisible line. All that anger dissipated just seeing Rob limited to a chair he had trouble getting out of.

"How's the case with the Johnson boy coming?"

"You been following it?"

"Whatever gets on the news I watch."

"He means that. He's a news junkie." Sylvia smiled at them both.

"Well, I can't say it's going that well. The guy is out there and we can't get to him."

"Patience. He'll fuck up at some point. They do you know."

"The patience part isn't working too well with the department. No results. It's killing me. Where's Deke?"

"He called about an hour ago. His son has a bad fever. He and Patti took him to the emergency room."

"Is he okay?"

"Just a bad flu. They over-reacted, that's what Deke said."

Dan looked closer at Rob. His bulk now was gone, replaced by a scarecrow body yet his voice still boomed. "It's good to see you. You are looking well. Better than last year."

"Sure. And I'm waiting for the big miracle to get me out of this."

"Are you getting around okay?"

"So far the meds are keeping it about right. It will get harder though. No illusions about that."

Sylvia came back in with a drink tray. "What can I get you?" They both took whiskeys, neat. Sylvia poured herself a glass of wine.

"How are you doing?" Dan asked her. Then he realized this was her life now. She'd given up her job as a bank manager to stay home and take care of her husband. Dan didn't know what that entailed though she seemed cheerful enough. They made small talk until it was time for dinner, followed by gifts and cake. Sylvia had made a big effort and more than anything Dan missed the presence of Deke and his wife

**

Aaron Clark could be in New York or he could be anywhere in the world though technically it would be difficult to get anywhere other than Mexico or Canada without raising suspicion. Clark was an amateur who somehow had come up with a fake ID, but hadn't gotten to the point of stealing credit cards. With the little Dan knew about him, he couldn't picture Clark managing credit card theft though desperation had its consequences.

Dan hoped Clark wouldn't know how to get a fake passport so the chances of his appearing abroad would be limited. Nothing could be discounted. The fact Clark had stuck around made it possible they could catch up with him. And the money would run out at some point.

Thanks to CSI everyone now knew the basics of DNA. Dan wondered how many criminals had benefited from the bits of information gathered from TV and the internet. They knew if they doused a place with bleach it would wipe out most everything.

Deke popped his head in. "Sorry about the dinner."

"How's Jason?"

"Better. Gave us a hell of a scare."

"Is he home?"

"Yeah. Patti's off work to stay with him. Pneumonia's not like it used to be. Killed my grandfather. Now it's like having a bad cold."

"Sounds pretty serious to me."

"Patti's a worrier, that's all. Antibiotics and rest."

"Well, I'm glad he's ok." Dan made a mental note to pick up a Manga book for him. "You were missed."

"Sure. I'm the life of the party; I'll drop by to see Rob one of these days after work. Meeting at 10 in Cheryl's office. Don't be late."

***

Cheryl turned to Dan. "What have you got?"

"The travelling Visa card. It's in New York now."

Deke couldn't resist, "We could go down. Take in a show."

Cheryl didn't crack a smile. "We have got to get a break."

***

Back in his office, Dan called Maggie. "Maggie, would a woman be trying to get pregnant and not tell the man?"

"I suppose it happens. Wait a minute. Don't tell me. Jess."

Dan explained. "Maybe this is what it's all about."

"That doesn't make sense. Couldn't it just be an accident?"

"Well, I don't feel like seeing her anymore." Dan sounded like a child.

"Come on Dan. No little Danny's around for Auntie Maggie."

"Don't joke. I am way too old for that."

"In Hollywood you'd still be young."

"They have money and time. I can barely get through the day. Plus I don't know what to think about Jess now."

"Are you in love with her?"

"I don't know. This was a scare."

"You could give her the benefit of the doubt. Weren't you in love with her before you found the test?"

"I really have no idea."

"I'm sorry. I wanted this to be good for you."

"I know."

"Have you talked to her about it?"

"Well, I am still too pissed off for the big talk."

Chapter Ten

That night Dan had the dream again. He was in a car with a woman behind the wheel. Was it Miranda or Jess? The car veered out of control and was heading straight for a tree. Dan woke with a start, gasping for breath. He got up and splashed water on his face. It had felt so real. The car was picking up speed and the big solid oak loomed directly ahead. Dan was afraid to go back to sleep; fearing the dream would just continue. But what if it did? It was just a dream. He could let it go. Dan wondered if he did, would he find out what really was waiting for him? But at four in the morning that thought was weighing heavily.

Dan shivered. Jess would lead him to death, more than any other woman would. Jess equaled Miranda and Jess had fooled him all along. He expected her to be the light that negated all the darkness, like a child's simple fears dissipated with the flick of a light switch. But no, Jess had her own strange world which Dan couldn't understand or even believe in. Jess's world was less penetrable and darker than Miranda's drinking had been. What could be blacker than communing with the dead on a regular basis?

"Get a grip." These were not the thoughts that would get him back to sleep. Dan picked up a Sudoku magazine and tried to lose himself in numbers. That's what Jess had said; numbers were the things farthest removed from ghosts and bad dreams.

Dan was just falling asleep when the alarm rang. He might as well not have slept at all. Another day, another dollar as his father would say. Dan tried not to look too closely at his face. He'd had better days and this one had barely begun. He rooted around the medicine cabinet for some B vitamins. This was his end of winter with the

Miranda depression and from the looks of it, it was going to be a doozy.

"The gym," he said. "I've got to get to the gym." His stomach felt flabby. More crunches and weights. If he could squeeze in the time, he'd go today.

There was enough cereal in the bottom of three boxes to make a bowl. He ate it slowly and then downed the vitamins. One cup of coffee. He made the good stuff, grinding it fresh and pouring it through a filter. He wouldn't have to pick up a cup at Tim Horton's on his way downtown.

What could he do if he stopped being a cop? This was a question that occurred to him at least once a week but he was too far from retirement and too late for a new career. There was always the option of being a security officer in the Middle East. "Right. Go directly to hell. Don't pass go. Bombs and oil. Death all around. Stacked up in piles all around you." If he survived an experience like that, which was a big if, he might not be in any shape to retire. Maybe he could just move to a small town like Joey had done. How much crime could there be in Warsaw? He tried to envision that alternative reality, greeting neighbors as he walked a beat like in an episode of Andy Griffith.

The phone rang. Dan took a deep breath before he answered it. It was Jess who acted as if nothing had happened. "I haven't seen Chris at all since I took her to school that morning. She's at Craig's mom's."

"Is that good?"

"I'm not sure. At least it's not boarding school."

"Not yet anyway. Did you get your lawyer on it? Jess, let me know what happens. I'm running late. I've got to get my ass to work."

"Can I see you?"

"Sure."

"When?"

There was no way to avoid seeing Jess. "Tomorrow after work. Is that good?"

"I'll stop by."

***

As soon as he got to his office, Deke popped in. "Any news?"

"Still stuck at zero. God, I'm sick of saying that."

"It's gotta break. The photos out. The New Yorkies are on it. But you know, Cheryl is cutting my time on this case. Too much else out there."

***

Maggie called, "He wants children."

It took Dan a minute to work out who his sister was talking about. "Who? Oh, your new beau. What? You've got kids. He knows that. He can have an instant family. What more does he want?"

"I'm too old. Men are just so stupid. He even said we could adopt. The amazing thing is I've even considered it." Maggie's voice almost broke.

"I'm sorry. Really I am. I know you liked him."

"Why didn't I meet him ten years ago?"

"Maggie, let me take you to dinner. How about a nice hot Vietnamese soup? That'll help." For years that was how he and Maggie solved problems. A meal was always a part of their ritual and by the end of it, they usually felt better even if nothing had been resolved.

They met at the small restaurant downtown near City Hall. "Magpie." Dan gave her a hug. They moved into a booth.

"I could use a drink."

"No license here."

"Damn."

"We'll get one after."

Maggie was quieter than usual and the soup kept them busy adding basil leaves and bean sprouts. Out of habit Maggie stopped Dan from adding hot peppers. "You'll regret that."

"You're right but let me enjoy it."

"So you tell me about Jess."

"No, you first."

"There's nothing more to say. That was it. We won't go on. He missed having a family and he says that's what he really wants now."

"Asshole. How old is he anyway?"

"Your age. I hadn't thought of babies in years. That chaos, the bottles, the attention, all of it came back. You're so busy you can't pick up a book for the first eight years. You know the worst of it?" Dan waited a moment. "I wouldn't even mind. That is if I could. I can't do it." She went on, "But there's the scent of the baby, milk, the soft little head. God, I have got to stop. I'm making myself crazy."

"If you really wanted to... a surrogate."

"I don't want it that much. I may be nostalgic. If I never had kids, maybe, but you know how exhausting it is?"

"I have some idea." Dan smiled, remembering his nephews when they were little. "And that's not what I want either."

"And Jess does?"

"I'm not sure. Maybe you're right and it was just a scare. I can't really tell what she's thinking. What if she were with me just to get pregnant?"

"She's so into having a baby with a cop's genes that she'll do anything you mean?"

"You tell me. I don't know get it."

"I can't speak for Jess. But as for me, I've already left my genetic material here on earth. Maybe it's not such a bad idea for you." Maggie teased.

"On a physical level your genetic material can die out at some point even with offspring. The point is you live on in the people who remember you."

"Good or bad. But in your case...." Maggie left Miranda's name unspoken.

***

Dan worked on getting his tie straight. Since he met Jess, he'd begun to pay attention to how he looked. He was waking up from a long winter slumber and feeling like Rip Van Winkle. Years had passed and he hadn't moved on. In fact, he was still been wearing the same clothes. Yes, he'd give Jess credit for that change.

Dan fit the cop mold; he could be tough on the outside. The dark grey suit was his mainstay and it was plain enough not to stick out. Every time he put it on he was reminded of Miranda who had gone with him to pick it out. "Time to put this sucker to rest." Dan said to himself.

***

Those first moments in the courtroom were unnerving. Dan took a deep breath as he was called to take the stand. It was one of those cases you never forgot. A young woman had drowned her baby in the bathtub for no apparent reason; she was well-off and her clothes screamed money. The defense was aiming for insanity but Dan doubted it would work. All the jury needed was a photo of the baby the way Dan had seen him.

Dan looked out over a big crowd. The media had latched on to the story and refused to let go. Even the national press was here to get the scoop, rich girl drowns baby in despair.

"Tell the jury what you saw when you arrived at the house."

Dan could almost see the pool and smell the chlorine. The paramedics were trying to resuscitate the baby. He described it best he could.

"Were there signs of this death being intentionally caused?"

"There were signs the baby had struggled."

"Wouldn't there be those signs if the baby fell in the pool by accident?"

"The forensic report showed different water in the lungs. Not chlorinated pool water. Just regular tap water."

This piece of evidence was obviously new to many of the observers as a murmur rose in the courtroom. "The baby was drowned in the bathtub, then taken to the pool to make it look like an accident."

"Objection. That is speculation."

Dan looked at Mrs. Evans. She sat straight staring out in front of her. On the day of the drowning, she had been hysterical, crying and screaming her baby was dead. Someone took her into the house but she'd resisted every step.

Dan wanted to describe how distraught she was but no one asked him. Something about the mom made him feel sympathetic, understanding she had crossed some point losing control. There were cases of postpartum depression that led to terrible consequences. The prosecutor nodded as Dan left the courtroom.

It was a short walk over to the precinct. The air was finally warming up. Dan carried his overcoat on his arm. This winter had dragged on so long he'd almost given up hope of ever feeling warm again.

But instead of entering the station, Dan walked down to the marina and continued to the river. It was April and the river carried the remains of the lake ice left when the ice boom had been lifted. Chunks of grey ice floated by and the breeze off the river carried its chill. The Niagara River was a special place for Dan. It was the only place he'd glimpsed the person his father could have been, rather than the angry, small minded man who made them all miserable.

On fishing Saturdays, his father would prepare sandwiches and they'd walk on the break-wall. Mostly they fished in silence and it was those moments that Dan could appreciate now. It was the only way his father could connect with him.

Today he was going to see Jess. He tugged on his tie to loosen it get it off. He had a thick neck and hated the restriction of a tie. It felt like it choked off his oxygen supply. Sitting on a bench staring at the current carrying the ice away, Dan had the sense that something of himself was now flowing and moving. Ice and cold, the constrictions of his life could melt away.

***

"So what's the latest on the Visa card?" Dan stopped by Cheryl's office.

"Nothing new. We've got everyone on the lookout. No one is expecting much. It is New York after all; he can hide out pretty well in a city that big."

***

Aaron Clark stepped out of the men's room in Penn Station. He couldn't believe he was back again. He hated New York; everything about it made him nervous, the noise, the taxis, the crowds, even the air itself. It was April but the wind was icier than in Buffalo. He really wished he had gone to the islands but he wasn't the kind of person who travelled to tropical places. At least here everyone had a white winter look, not like Miami where bronzed people stared at him like there was something wrong. Here in New York, Aaron fit in. He varied his walks each day; New York was a perfect spot for not being noticed.

***

By the time Dan got his desk cleared off, it was after five. "What the hell am I doing with my time? Why is my desk still full after hours of work?" Those were the questions that never had an answer.

Dan looked at his watch. Jess was due to show up and already his stomach was hurting. The phone rang. "I'm sorry, Dan. I've got to pick up Chris at her grandmother's and then I really need to spend some time with her. You don't mind too much, do you? I'll call you tomorrow."

Dan couldn't have been more relieved. He got up and poured himself another cup of coffee and got back to the computer.

"Coward." He said to himself, but he smiled.

Deke poked his head in. "Dan, my man. You are calling out for a beer. Get that coffee out of your hand."

"How'd you know?"

"I got these powers."

If he believed in Jess's world, Deke was his guardian angel. They stopped at a downtown bar, blending in with the after work crowd. The kids would be invading later but for now it was a pretty sedate, people winding down from their workaday world.

Deke had one beer and begged off, "Have to get home. You know how it is. My kids. Jason is better but I should get home."

"Go on, get out of here." Dan ordered one more because he hadn't been out in a bar like this in a very long time and he didn't feel like going home. He needed a break from the case and thinking about Jess. Two women were standing next to him and the one closest to him said, "We were trying to figure out what you do."

Dan played along. "I help people."

The first woman was a bottle blonde, friendly and talkative. The outline of her large breasts showed through her sweater. "And I save lives."

"You're a doctor." Dan had had just enough to of a buzz so that the women were blurry and appealing. Her friend was pretty, with dark hair, dark eyes. Maybe Jess had left an imprint on him because for years he sought out women who resembled Miranda. At least now he wasn't looking for an imitation.

The blonde laughed. "I'm a designer. Mostly I do offices, but sometimes houses."

"Can I get you something to drink?"

She looked at her friend and nodded. "I'm Sherrie and this is Claudia."

He held out his hand. "I'm Dan." He didn't want to say what he did in case they bolted or were too interested.

"What plans do you have for a Friday night?" he asked.

"To get totally wasted."

"Sounds good." Dan finished his third beer and felt positively cheerful. Then Sherrie ordered margaritas. The second one sent him to the men's room where he doubled over and vomited bile. He needed to get some food into his stomach. He washed his face. Hell, he wasn't a teenager anymore.

For years he'd prided himself on holding his booze but those days were definitely over. With Miranda he'd had to control himself somewhat since at the end of the night she was the one who needed to be taken care of. A bit unsteady on his feet, he checked his clothes and rinsed his mouth out vigorously and popped two antacids. He hoped the women would be gone but no such luck.

"I think I'll be heading home." Dan said trying to straighten up.

Claudia looked less drunk than Sherrie. "Should you drive?"

"Sure, I'll be ok."

"We can go over to the Towne and get something to eat."

Dan felt better after an omelet and home fries. "This was a great idea." After his second coffee he felt ready to leave. "Will you be okay?" He asked. "Can I give you a lift?"

Sherrie had left the table to talk to a group of friends at a big table in the center of the room. It was only ten but Dan felt like it was closer to 4 AM and reminded him of the times he had gone out with Miranda. Claudia went over to talk to her friend and when she came back, she said, "Sherrie's staying. They're friends of hers so yes, I'll take a ride if you don't mind."

"You just have to direct me."

"I live in Tonawanda. Are you sure you're okay?"

"The food helped." She wouldn't want to know he'd puked half the booze out of his system. He managed the drive slowly with his full concentration though he felt exhausted.

"I'll get you some more coffee." Claudia offered when they arrived.

The house was just perfect, beautiful with hard wood floors and simple furniture. It was a place Dan would have lived in if he'd had another life. "Your house is beautiful."

"Thank you."

"I've been seeing someone. It isn't going well but I don't know what's going to happen. Otherwise..." Dan left the sentence unfinished. "How come you're not wasted?"

"I only had about half of what you both had."

Dan's eyelids were closing. "I need to get home before I fall asleep right here."

"Stay."

He kissed her. They got their clothes off and then what seemed like in a matter of seconds, she was on top of him doing all the work. When he came he felt it like an explosion in his brain.

When he woke the next morning, the night came back to him in a series of flashes, some of which made him cringe. His arm was flung over her. Her body was the color of honey in the morning light. Dan turned his head and kissed her shoulder, the part of her body closest to his lips.

She woke, "Oh my head."

"Aspirin?"

"In the bathroom." Dan brought her the aspirin and water. No signs of modesty, she looked at him without looking away, not covering herself up."Thanks."

Dan said, "I should go."

"Make some coffee. How can you be so…"

"Chipper?"

"And I feel like hell."

The comforter had ended up on the floor. "Are you cold?" Dan picked it up and pulled it over her.

"Come back. It's cold out there."

Dan touched her breasts. "Is this okay?"

She nodded. "Please."

***

While she was showering, Dan started on making coffee and toast. Everything seemed to be easy. Claudia emerged in a soft white robe. "So what's up with your girlfriend?"

"I don't know."

"We never found out what it is you do last night. Top secret?"

"I'm a cop. A detective."

"I thought so."

"Is it that obvious?"

"No, but I have a cousin who's a cop so I see certain signs."

"Here?"

"No, he's in New York. You don't have to worry."

"And what do you do? I remember the night in kind of flashes."

"I'm an architect."

"That's why this is such a nice place."

"It was originally my grandmother's house. I had it gutted and redid the inside."

"It makes me feel like I want to live here." Dan realized that didn't come out the way he'd planned. "I mean…"

"I have a great garden out back with a meditation pool but that'll have to wait since it's pretty much of a mud soup. Plus everything is still kind of brown but in a few weeks it should be glorious. In the summer I'm always out there."

"Do you do get work around here?"

"Some houses, sometimes shopping centers, and a big housing project in Toronto. I travel too. I'm from here so this is my base. I grew up in this house."

"You don't expect to see all this light in a house. You've done a great job." Dan paused for a moment. "Are you seeing anyone?"

"Not at the moment. I am so busy with my work."

"I know how you feel." Then Dan asked, "Did you have fun last night?"

"Sherrie wanted to celebrate. It's her 40th so it was my turn to take her out. I'm really out of practice. I'm not a big drinker and I don't do bars much. Do you?"

"Not for years though you wouldn't know that from last night. I'm in a strange kind of place in my life. If I weren't in the middle of," Dan stopped because he didn't even know how to define it. "I really would love to see you again."

"How do you know I'd like to see you?"

"I don't. Why would you? Tequila, let's see, a girlfriend that I'm not sure what to do about. Hey, I'm the perfect guy to go out with."

Claudia laughed. "Look, it's okay. We had a good time. Don't worry about it. If some day it doesn't work out with your girlfriend and I'm not involved..."

Dan gave her his card and took hers. He put it carefully in his wallet. What he felt for the first time in months was a sense of peace

***

On his way home, Dan got a call on a possible arson case with two deaths, a father and son. Clarisse was there already, talking to the neighbors. The ashes were still too hot for anyone except the fire department to handle. "A four alarmer." Clarisse greeted him. "You look like you had one hell of a night."

"See anything?"

"You mean like gasoline soaked rags?" Clarisse lifted her eyebrows and shook her head.

"How'd they die?" Dan tried again.

"Smoke inhalation. Think they were dead drunk or they would've woke up."

"So its arson?"

"Just a guess. They've been trying to burn down this neighborhood for years to build condos. So Dan, were you out last night? Did you? You know?"

"You're worse than Deke."

Dan got home in the afternoon. There was shopping to do, calls to make, but Dan only wanted to eat and crawl into bed. He called in an order for wonton soup and lo mein. Just as he was sitting down in front of the TV with the food, Todd walked in.

"Good timing." Dan pointed to his cartons. "Get a plate."

"Thanks. Got any beer?"

"Check on the porch." Dan usually kept a case out on the back porch through the cold months. "Bring me one. See your mom lately?"

"Last night."

"Is she okay?"

"Sure. Do we have to watch that shit?" Todd pointed at the home repair channel.

Dan threw him the remote.

"No movies?" Todd asked.

"You've probably seen them all."

Todd rummaged around his backpack. "I brought one. Sci fi. "Dark City.""

"Talk about being set up." Dan sank back in his chair, not knowing what was in store.

"You'll love it; it's like film noir. You're not going to sleep on me."

"No way." Dan lied, already feeling the warmth of the food catch up with him.

"Did you have a bad day?"

"No."

"You look tired. I can go. It's ok."

"No, stay, you know that."

"I'm going down to Cornell to see Sean."

"Great."

"I don't know. It's kind of snobby."

"Not your brother; he's cool."

"I don't know his girlfriend."

"You can fill us in on all the dirt." Dan wished he could inject some confidence into his nephew. "If you want, take my car." Todd looked at him in disbelief. "Just bring it back, no scratches with a full tank of gas." Dan wasn't even sure if Todd's old Dodge would make the six hour trip to Ithaca.

"Thanks. Are you sure?"

Dan nodded. "Just leave me yours. Maybe the car elves will have a look at it while you're gone."

"What'd you do? Have a big night out?"

"Why do you ask?"

"You have that hangover thing going on. Look at you, man. Talk about dark circles. How's the girlfriend?"

"I don't know."

"What'd you mean you don't know?"

"Maybe that's a way of knowing."

"Don't get all Zen on me. Hey, I didn't meet her. I can tell if she's good for you."

"I'll remember that."

"Could you tell mom not to bake anything for Sean? I can't take anything with me."

"Sure."

***

Aaron Clark woke drenched in sweat. He'd been dreaming, someone was holding his head down into a pool of water. He rubbed his eyes and then he remembered. His stepfather delivered all manners of punishment. One of them was to stick Aaron's head in the toilet and keep flushing.

Chapter Eleven

By ten on Sunday morning Dan had already worked out at the gym. He held his cell in his hand, ready to call Jess but he just couldn't bring himself to do it. Deke's call snapped him out of his reverie. "He's had an accident."

Dan didn't need to ask who. "Bad?"

"A bike crashed into him."

"And that caused an injury?"

"They ride like maniacs in New York. He tried to get away but he sprained his ankle or maybe worse."

"Wait, run that by me again. This man we've been tracking for months is just walking down the street and gets hit by a bike."

"Crossing a street. The bike ran the light, top speed. Get the picture."

"So he's in custody."

"Not exactly. He was lying on the ground when the ambulance came. As soon as he could get up, he took off."

"Hobbling away."

"The cop there thought that was odd and checked around for his picture and there you have it. Too late."

"Where is he?"

"That we don't know."

"They let him get away. I can't believe it. How hard could it have been? Now he's hobbling around Manhattan."

"He was born under a lucky star. Dan, just don't get pissed at Hunter."

Dan got the number and talked to Hunter, the beat cop who witnessed the accident. "You let him get away."

"There was no suspicion. He was a victim. I figured maybe he didn't have insurance or something."

"So then, what made you decide to check?" Dan tried to control the tone of his voice so as not to let any sarcasm slip in.

"He was in one hurry. Not normal with that kind of injury. Hell, most of us would need a serious dose of painkillers to move around like that. His ankle could be broken."

"You're checking the clinics, the hospitals."

"Of course. So far, nothing."

**

Aaron Clark hauled himself up the stairs with the help of the railing. He was in a 6th floor walkup he found online. He didn't think his ankle was broken but damn it hurt. He stepped off the curb to cross the street and the asshole on the bike plowed right into him. When he got up his entire leg blazed with pain. He finally sat down on the steps, exhausted. He tried sitting on the steps, then going ass backwards one step at a time.

He'd spent two thousand for this shithole of a place. Who would have thought there were still buildings with no elevator? Where was the progress in America? Wasn't this the 21st century?

With these prices he'd be out of cash fast enough. At least there was a Chinese restaurant that delivered right to his door. He wouldn't starve but he was getting tired of greasy rice and soup. He stocked up on Nyquil, Advil, Benadryl, and every other painkiller he could come up with. They weren't making too much of a dent but at least with the Nyquil at least he could sleep a little. He wondered if he could get anything stronger but he couldn't draw any more attention to himself.

He never stopped checking the news but there was nothing about him or the kid, not since the mother gave up pleading for help. He smiled now to think of the futility of those pleas. "Hell, I could do a better job pleading the case myself."

A few minutes more and he was pulling himself up to the door and finally to the apartment. The Advil was wearing off and he wanted to scream. The owner hadn't left much behind but there was a bottle of peach schnapps and one of whiskey. Aaron took a slug of the schnapps. The taste was sticky and furry. He made it to the couch. Next to him was a coffee can he'd been peeing into. He needed to save his strength. So this is what it had come to?

***

"Dan, I'd like you to do more in the community. Try to be more visible." Cheryl had called Dan into her office. They sat facing each other drinking coffee.

It was the last thing he'd expected to hear. There was no progress on the case, one of the officers, an old friend, was facing sexual harassment charges and Cheryl was telling him this. Dan was speechless.

"Why don't you think about it? Run for sheriff or a position in city hall. The problem is Dan, you have to try for those jobs. Make a bit of an effort."

"You mean, suck up."

"Public appearances don't hurt. Look like you're part of us here."

He was wondering where this was leading. "Cheryl, I have absolutely no interest. I have no political ambitions. You know that."

"It's not just that. It's image. We need to improve our image. You know how much negative press we get. We need to look better, so there's a positive association when the public thinks of us. None of the brutality and harassment."

"We're working on it. We've got officers on bikes in the park; we're doing career days at schools. You know all the workshops for the officers."

"I mean cultural activities. We need to look like we actually pick up a book from time to time and read."

"I'm a detective. What does it matter what I do? You want me to join the Philharmonic or something?"

Friday, there's a special opening at the Albright Knox. The governor, all the big wigs will be there."

"Art isn't my thing. But honestly I can't imagine why anyone would care if I went to an opening." Cheryl frowned and Dan quickly added, "I didn't say I wouldn't go. I just don't see the point."

This would be his opportunity for that talk with Jess. He'd never been to an opening and had no idea what he was supposed to do there, if anything at all. As he suspected, Jess was happy to hear from him and delighted to go.

Dan was social enough but this was out of his range. He'd been to the Gallery as a child, and a few times with Miranda who loved painting and wanted to convince Dan that it could be fun. Somehow it never worked and he ended up sitting on a bench in front of a painting waiting until she got tired enough to want to go home.

When he got to the museum, he found Jess upstairs already holding a glass of wine. As always, she looked beautiful but tonight she had put her long hair up which made her look more sophisticated. Dan felt a mixture of desire and guilt at seeing her. She was smiling, happy to see him. "We don't have to stay long," he assured her.

"I just got here. Let's look around. It's a great museum."

They stopped in front of Gauguin's Yellow Christ. "Now he was quite the romantic figure."

"Yes, he was." Jess smiled. "You know the artists."

"Everyone knows Gauguin." Dan had seen a documentary about his life years ago. It had stuck with him, the way the artist escaped to Tahiti leaving behind his wife and family. It took a courage that Dan knew he didn't possess. Either courage or madness.

Upstairs there was a show of conceptual art. "I'm lost here." Dan said to Jess.

"Me too."

People were milling about in one of the small galleries off the larger room. Dan recognized a state senator. What was Cheryl's idea? Was he supposed to go and chat with a complete stranger? Was he supposed to get in a picture with the mayor?

He spotted Claudia standing next to a sculpture, talking to two men. She was moving her hands animatedly. Dan felt his stomach drop. She was dressed in a turquoise top making her stand out in a room of women in black.

Jess was peering into a glass case of Picasso sculptures. Claudia caught sight of Dan and smiled. Dan wished he had come alone. Jess, who looked up at that precise moment, turned to Dan, "Do you know her?"

"A friend." Dan answered.

"She's attractive, for an older woman."

Dan and Jess paused in front of a multi-colored installation. Dan looked closer, "Hey, check this out. Those are coffee creamer things. Someone actually emptied these and filled each one of them up with paint."

Jess looked closer. "How long would that take?"

"Look at the colors. It's kind of cool."

***

Aaron Clark bound up his ankle with a bandage and got ready for his trip to the drugstore. He'd been putting it off, but he had no more painkillers left. The pain wasn't as sharp as it was a couple of days ago but it was constant. He got down the stairs again by step sitting on his ass. He'd counted 72, each with a painful jostle of his body as he positioned it to move to the next. When he got to the landing, he hauled himself up by the railing and wanted to cry.

Once outside he tried not to call attention to himself by hobbling too noticeably. It took every bit of his will to stand straight. In the drugstore on the corner he found more Nyquil and Advil. He also picked up Epsom salts; when he was a kid with a sprained ankle his mother had him soak his foot. He wanted to include some food but it had to be easy to carry so he settled for two cans of tuna, chips, and some cookies. The cashier looked up at him, "Got a sprain?"

Aaron nodded.

"They can hurt like hell."

"A pack of Marlboros." He hoped the cigarettes could help distract him from the pain. The cashier rang up the total. He told himself he could do it; there were climbers who made it off mountaintops with broken limbs. This was nothing in comparison.

Back on the street, he tried to keep his mouth from twisting in a grimace of pain. He would call for Chinese takeout again. Maybe he could find a grocery that delivered. Being trapped in that tiny space was making him paranoid. They could be waiting for him at any moment, and there would be nothing he could do. He could barely get down the stairs.

The trip had taken just over an hour and left him exhausted. He soaked his foot in the bathtub which took some maneuvering. When he got out, he felt better. It had been a few days since he'd been able to bathe. He needed a haircut too; he was starting to look unkempt.

Aaron Clark got back on the couch. He'd never been much of a TV watcher but now he was watching every series ever made, including old Bonanza episodes that he had hated as a child. His stepfather never missed a single one. Now he had to admit they beat the reality shows that were cruel, each person was out to get the other, no matter what. It didn't matter if they were sharing a house or competing for a date; there were no holds barred. No wonder the world was in a sorry state. He smiled at the absurdity of that, he'd made his own contribution.

When he closed his eyes, sometimes he saw the boy, the body limp after he gave him a coke with the sleeping pills in it. At least the kid didn't feel a thing. He'd never gone so far before. And now, this was the price he had to pay.

***

A chaste kiss goodnight and Dan left Jess off at her door with an excuse of having to be up very early. He felt like an unfaithful married man. All those years with Miranda he was never unfaithful; he never knew what to expect next and that kept the excitement level, or the tension high enough that he never strayed.

She had exactly two incidents she blamed on booze. There wasn't much Dan could say to Miranda when she was crying, out of control, begging him not to be so mad at her. It meant nothing, there was only him she repeated over and over. In the end, he believed her; she was so beautiful, how could he be surprised when someone else found her to be? The fact was he couldn't imagine how not to be with her, even as awful as her betrayals got.

When he found out about the first one, Miranda couldn't do enough. She would never drink again; she would change everything if only Dan would believe her. And after the second time, there was more of the same. Miranda on best behavior was as hard to take as her drunken evil twin. That was her joke; it wasn't her at all but someone she had no control of. Miranda tried so hard, cooking his favorite meals, buying him presents like pieces of clothing or nice chocolates. There hadn't been a third occasion but probably would have been if fate hadn't intervened.

They would have ended up separating. Sometimes Dan wondered if he had stayed because he was afraid to leave her on her own or if it was his own fear of being alone. But if he'd let her reach bottom, maybe now she'd be alive. That's what all the stories on alcoholism said, but in those days Dan didn't know this and even if he had, he was in the thick of it, living it as intensely as she had.

Dan had managed to cut down on drinking and just maybe, Miranda would never have been able to. What kind of future would that have been? Dan didn't often let his mind go there; he preferred the rosy picture his mind had created over the years with the beautiful Miranda.

It could have been precisely that ease which she was seeking with the drinking, to feel comfortable with herself. He'd never delved into her psyche when she was alive so all of those questions remained unanswered all these years. Did he even know if she had been happy? Maybe she never lived up to her prom queen image he discovered was part of her. That was a Miranda he had never known and it may have been what she'd tried to be, a perfect woman, not a real one, erased and defined by her own beauty.

So why wasn't a new life possible for him now? Deke had a family; why couldn't Dan? It was becoming clear to Dan that that wasn't going to be with Jess. It wasn't even the pregnancy scare as much as he simply wasn't in love with her. Once things were straight with Chris, Dan would tell her. Maybe he wouldn't even have to; she was the psychic after all.

That night Dan had the dream again. This time it was a car in the snow version of the guardrail dream. He woke, drenched in sweat, his mouth in the shape of a scream. 5 AM. He might as well get up. He put the cross streets of the bicycle accident on Google Earth. Aaron Clark had to still be in the general vicinity.

New York police had checked the shops in the area but these days it was hard to get clear information. People were no longer tuned into the outside world much at all.

They missed what was right under their noses; between their cell phones and iPods, they saw only their screens. And in New York, tuning out was a survival technique; for many the point was to block out the exterior world. The only thing that was certain was that Aaron Clark was injured and an officer had spoken to him.

Dan could do it himself. A trip to New York wasn't out of the question. He could book a flight and make the rounds of the neighborhood himself. He needed to act.

When he called Deke from the airport, Deke was pissed. "Wait a minute. After Miami, you're going to New York. Why didn't you tell me? I'd come with you."

"It's Sunday. Spend the day with your kids."

***

While Dan was waiting in the airport, Jess called. "You know, I can tell something's wrong." Dan was silent, trying to think of a response. "I know you don't believe me, but I wasn't trying to get pregnant."

"It's not that." He managed.

"Is it something to do with that woman we saw last night?"

"No. Not at all." There was the general buzz of the airport around him. "Jess, I care about you but I just don't think it will work out."

"Why not? I thought we were doing fine."

"Well, on certain levels it wasn't working."

"You want to try to be a little more vague about that?"

"I'm at the airport. I've got to go." He was taking the easy way out.

Dan could almost taste the moment when he would take Clark into custody. When he landed at LaGuardia, he called the head of the precinct.

It was a slow Sunday afternoon and Dan took a cab into the city. Every time he'd ever come to New York, he felt the excitement of Manhattan. Like a country bumpkin coming to the big city, he felt his nasal Buffalo accent get stronger. The officer who'd talked to Clark had agreed to meet with him and was waiting for Dan. "Tim Hunter," he shook Dan's hand.

Dan had come with his street maps of the area all laid out. Tim pushed them aside. "The blocks are all square. Easy as pie."

"Tell, me what you've checked so far."

"Got the boys out there yesterday. Do you know how many people live in those blocks?"

"Got to start somewhere."

"Well, let's get to it."

They started out at the end of the block from the accident. There was a diner, a dry cleaner's, and a Chinese restaurant. No one reported anything, but that was a function of urban anonymity. They'd worked outward but by 6, Tim was ready to stop.

"Come on. One more block. They were standing in front of a Duane Reade drugstore. The clerk inside looked at the picture and nodded. "Sure. He came in about three days ago, limping something terrible. I asked him if he had a sprain but he didn't want to talk much. Bought plenty of Nyquil."

"So he could sleep," Dan wanted to shout. "Jackpot." He said it under his breath.

"You're certain."

"Yes, I don't usually work Thursdays and I was filling in. I got another job but the manager was short so what could I do? I can't afford to lose this."

Dan stood on the sidewalk with Officer Hunter, He noticed the trees covered in green buds. He never thought of New York as having any nature at all. "Mostly apartment buildings around here. Not many hotels in this neighborhood."

"He's got to be right here. He can hardly walk." Dan said.

They started on the buildings on each side of the street checking each one by one. Dan found an old man on the bottom floor apartment who was willing to talk. "I haven't seen him lately. Hurt his foot; could be resting." He called Hunter and they got to the top floor and buzzed repeatedly. Dan looked at the door, "Let's do it."

Tim Hunter gave him a nod. "Go for it." It was reinforced but after picking at it, Dan got the lock to flip open. Aaron Clark lay face down on the floor, next to the sofa with the television on. Dan listened for a pulse while Hunter called for an ambulance.

The room was disgusting. Urine overflowed containers. Empty bottles of Nyquil were all over the floor."

Dan asked the medics when they arrived, "How bad is he?"

"Can't tell yet ." The paramedic shrugged.

They waited until an ambulance took him to St. Luke's Hospital. Tim Hunter drove his car to the hospital and he and Dan stayed outside the emergency room door waiting for information. "We'll get a guard posted ASAP."

"Doesn't look like he'll be going anywhere."

"No. Funny what you can get in a drugstore can actually cause that much damage."

"I just had a case of an old woman who had a weird mix of scripts, OTC, and a natural remedy and she died."

"I'll think twice about dosing myself with Nyquil when I get my next cold."

"Hey, if it's the only thing that lets you sleep…" Dan was grateful to be making small talk with Tim. For the first time since Petey disappeared he could relax. This was it, the magic moment he had been waiting for now for months on end; he could go home with the burden lifted. He'd already called Cheryl and Deke; now it was just a question of getting Clark into custody as soon as he regained consciousness. The blood test to compare the DNA on the kid's clothes would be simple enough. "It's taking a while, isn't it?'

"They don't want to let us in. Protective of even of the worst of the lot; it's like we're the enemy."

Dan wondered who Clark would have to contact, was there anyone who would care he was here? "Coffee?" He asked Tim.

"Sure. It looks like we might be here for a while."

Dan got up to walk around a bit. He opened the door a crack and looked into the Clark's room. He could see three people around the bed. The activity didn't have the frenetic feel of an ER episode which he took that to be a good sign; it was either that or he was already dead. But then he wouldn't be the first person to die of a mix of OTC medicine. It would be too ridiculous.

Chapter Twelve

Aaron Clark opened his eyes to a dingy green room. For a moment he wasn't sure where he was but he sensed he was free. Even if he had died it would have been an improvement over that apartment. His head felt heavy as if he could barely turn it and his mouth was dry and furry.

"Mr. Clark. I'm Dr. Garcia. You're in St. Luke's Hospital."

Aaron tried to remember who Luke was in the Bible. Did he have anything to do with the Resurrection? He felt his aunt's presence in the room, smiling at him from the chair in the corner.

"Can you hear me?"

Aaron moved his mouth to speak but couldn't squeak out any words so he just nodded.

"You're going to be fine. There is no serious damage. We've got you on a drip to rehydrate. We've taped up the foot. We'll give you some time but there are two police officers outside waiting to talk to you."

Of course, the police. That was why he was in this mess. Aaron tried to focus but instead kept looking at the chair that was now empty. His aunt had disappeared.

***

Dan returned with two coffees. "Much better than what we've got at work."

"No way." Tim asked him, "Bet you thought you weren't going to solve this one."

"You're right. Too much time gone by and the trail gets cold. We were lucky; an old guy showed up and remembered the car. I should send VW a thank you for making those beetles."

"The new ones?"

"He was driving one. Sticks out like a sore thumb and that's from a guy who couldn't be more inconspicuous."

"Odd for a perp. They usually try to keep a low profile especially if they're preying on kids."

"Think it just got away from him. Only one other thing he was involved in and it didn't stick."

***

A nurse came to get them. "He may be a little bit out of it but he's conscious. I don't know how much information you'll get from him at this point."

A uniformed officer was standing guard outside the door. He was reading Clark his rights when Clark nodded off in the middle. "We're going to have to wait." Tim said. "It's almost over."

Dan couldn't put his finger on it but he felt uneasy but he needed to settle this once and for all. They went back to the waiting room and Dan settled in to phone his sister after calling the station. "I think it's over but I've got a feeling."

"Why?"

"Clark can't escape; he's lying in a hospital bed. He looks small, kind of helpless."

"Dan." Maggie's voice was impatient. "Come on. That was one horrific crime; don't forget that."

"Of course not. I must be tired, that's all. Really tired of this in every way possible."

"Well, you'll be home soon enough, so just hang on. You're almost finished. We'll celebrate when you get back."

Dan walked up and down the hall wondering just what they had given Clark that was making him sleep so much. He picked up his cell and called Maggie again, "I think I broke up with Jess."

"What?"

"In the airport. I didn't do it very well."

"Dan, you didn't. How much time did you spend with her and you dropped her on the phone from the airport? Are you kidding me? Call her and apologize."

"Maybe it's too late."

"You really are an ass. She was in love with you."

"I don't know that."

***

Tim Hunter was waiting for him in the hall. "I'm calling it a day. Clark is down for the count. Waiting around is not going to help. Just get back here early in the morning." He looked at Dan for a minute. "You got a place to stay?"

"I didn't think that far ahead."

"I'm at my mother's in Brooklyn. You can stay there."

"Thank you but that's not necessary."

"You sure? You'll pass up a good Sunday dinner."

Dan felt the fatigue through his body and realized finding a hotel at the last minute would be a hassle. "Hey, man, thanks. I appreciate it."

"No problem."

"If you're ever in Buffalo."

"Sure."

***

By seven the following morning, Dan was back at the hospital. Clark was being discharged into police custody. An officer sat outside the door. "He's up. He knows what's going to happen."

Dan went in and found another officer sitting by the bed. "You're the detective from Buffalo. We're ready to go. We read him his rights and now he's waiting for a lawyer."

Since it was such a high profile case, Dan imagined lawyers lining up for a chance at it. "A court appointed one?"

The officer shook his head. "He's been doing some research."

Dan turned his attention to Clark. "Good morning, Mr. Clark. It's been quite a while, hasn't it?" He was a skinny sorry sight. Clark looked small and pale against the sheets.

The first thing Clark said was, "It isn't what it seems."

"No? Tell me just what that is."

"When the lawyer gets here."

All Dan could do was wait some more. Clark was being discharged and then taken to the holding center to be arraigned. In the end Tim had been right, not much point to all the waiting. As soon as the news leaked, the press would be everywhere but for the moment the police officers had the chance to proceed quietly. Clark looked amazingly relaxed for a man on his way to prison.

***

"He's screaming innocence." Dan got on the phone to Deke.

"They always do." Deke answered.

"There might be something to it."

"Well, that's his lawyers deal now. Not for you to worry about now. I'd like to see someone get him off now."

Dan hung up the phone.

***

Dan wasn't the officer in charge of the questioning. He stood behind the two way mirror with Tim. Clark's lawyer was sitting at the table along with another officer. The statement was being recorded. Clark began, his voice calm and surprisingly deep for a small man."I was driving on

Maple Road and saw a child who had fallen in the snow. It was about quarter to four."

"What were you doing in the area?"

"I'd just come back from the mall. There's a computer shop and I had to pick up a microphone. I don't usually drive there but I thought it'd be a shortcut from my usual route. There was supposed to be more snow heading our way and I wanted to get home before it hit."

"What happened when you saw the child?"

"There was just a dark shape in the snow. I wasn't sure what it was. So I stopped the car and picked him up."

"Why didn't you take him to his home?"

"He couldn't tell me anything. He was shaking."

"Didn't you think he lived right there? Why else would he be on a road like that?'

"Honestly, it didn't occur to me. I figured he needed help so I put him in the car."

"Where did you take him?"

"I wasn't sure what to do so first I just put the heat on high and tried to get him warmed up."

"Then?"

"Then, I just drove. I wasn't sure what to do. He couldn't tell me where he lived. I didn't know what to do."

"Go on."

"And then, I felt this overwhelming pain .." Here Clark stopped. "He was so little, so vulnerable. I don't know what happened."

"Where did you go?"

"I just kept going to my house. And then." Clark was finding it difficult to go on.

"Is that when you violated the boy?"

"It wasn't supposed to be that. I didn't mean to do it. I don't remember anything about it."

"Did you penetrate him anally?"

"I don't know. My mind goes blank. I don't know if I touched him. I know I gave him a coke to drink."

***

Dan jumped out of his chair and left the room, his head pounding and his mouth dry. He went to the restroom to wash his face and take some deep breaths. When he came back Tim said to him. "Picked up the boy, did the deed and dropped him off in the snow. Pretty gruesome shit."

Dan raised his eyebrows. "Where?"

"Near the road not far from where he picked him up. But he claims that the kid was fine when he left."

"So he claims someone else picked up the kid and finished him off."

"Apparently."

"What do you think about that?"

"Bullshit."

"He's a strange type. Not much like anyone I've run across."

"Me neither."

"Abuse victim, maybe. That's pretty common but it doesn't lead to killing. How long are you keeping him down here?"

"Should be yours tomorrow as long as nothing else surfaces."

"I'm sorry. I don't know what happened. I just couldn't hear anymore."

Tim looked at him. "Hey, we all have our limits. This one is pretty sick so don't apologize."

***

Dan went back to his cheap hotel, cheap in appearance only since everything else about it was pricey. He didn't want to spend another night with Tim and his mother. The window looked out onto an alleyway, allowing only a sliver of light into the room, and Dan couldn't wrestle it open for some much needed oxygen. His head was pounding and the city aggravated his claustrophobia; Dan physically needed more space. He was angry at himself too. He must have looked the fool. No one would know he hadn't been able to handle hearing the details of a crime that he'd been following since November. He shook his head. "How stupid."

He even felt the Clark case slipping away. Dan hadn't been able to listen to what happened according to Clark. It was over for him if he couldn't do his part and get the whole story down. What kind of detective shut down at a crucial moment?

A child abused. His own nephews had been safe as far as Dan could tell. He'd read so many statistics, some stated that as many as 20% of all boys had been sexually abused and for girls the stats were much higher. Stats were one thing; what Clark had done to such a young child was quite another.

***

One more day, Dan said to himself. "Just one more day." He feared his own experience in the city wasn't going to be terribly different from Clark's holed up in that disgusting apartment.

New York had never held much allure for Dan. Miranda, however, loved Broadway musicals and frequented art museums. He wondered if there was any place in the world that wouldn't hold a connection to her. Walking by the MOMA on his way back to the hotel, he remembered seeing the Picassos with her, Miranda walking around the museum in her sky high happiness explaining to him all the details of the paintings she could. Even now she haunted this hotel room though she'd never set foot in it.

"See, Jess, you couldn't fight her." Dan said out loud. "No one can." This was it; he was going to live his life with her presence next to him or over his right shoulder or inside whatever part of his body it was that she still inhabited. His eyes filled with tears.

He pulled the bedspread off and lay down on top of the sheets. He'd had to buy a shirt, socks, and underwear since he'd never planned on being here for more than a day. Now Deke could accuse him of going on a big city shopping spree.

He'd finished off the contents of whiskey in the mini bar and would have to start on vodka, his last resort. Vodka was his father's drink. He thought he could disguise the smell on his breath by only drinking white booze as he called it. That was reason enough for Dan to never touch it. He preferred dark rum and whiskey which gave him the hangovers from hell but kept the illusion he wasn't his father.

No, Dan was different. He never yelled at Miranda or kept the household in a constant state of tension. Or had he? Miranda never complained and there had been plenty of reasons. For one, there was the fact that Dan wasn't what she wanted. She was much smarter than he was. They fell into a mad lust and played it out for as long as it lasted, abetted by drink. Their sex life started to unravel precisely when Dan cut back. Maybe his inhibitions crept back or he no longer wanted to be with a drunk.

Dan wasn't a person who read many books or went to museums or knew much about high culture. He watched sports, visited his nephews, and went out partying on weekends. When Miranda woke up from their sex fueled fantasy, what did she think? That all her dreams were shattered? They shared the dream of children and Dan really believed he would have made a good father. Miranda must have thought so too, but that was the one thing that didn't happen.

***

Miranda should have been an actress; she was beautiful and outgoing. That might have been enough for her, the attention and adoration. Dan couldn't provide enough nor could the parameters of her teaching life no matter how great her students thought she was. He bowed his head down. He shouted it out loud. "Stop." The room seemed quieter than before with just the hum of the mini fridge and the underlying motor of the systems that kept the building inhabitable. "Just stop." He shouted again. All this time and there was no way out. He wondered what could get the brain to stop its incessant loop that always led to Miranda.

"Damn. Damn. Damn. Even here, even now. We're not even in Buffalo for God's sake. We were only here once. Leave me alone." Then he said it more plaintively, "Please." He curled up on the side of the bed away from the window, in a fetal position.

"Get the fuck up."

Miranda groaned and shook her head.

"Get up. I mean it."

No response. Dan felt rage build up and then he couldn't stop himself. He pulled her up off the sofa and shook her." Her body moved like an inanimate object, heavily swinging from side to side.

Finally she muttered, "You fucking asshole. Stop it."

Dan slapped her across the face and then didn't stop. Over and over until she crouched on the floor in a bundle pleading, "Stop it, please." Then she sobbed, big wet gasps that came from deep inside.

This was what it was like. Dan started to cry, here in this hotel room he could remember all of it, all that he'd been trying to erase.

Chapter Thirteen

Dan accompanied Clark onto the plane. This was a high profile case or they would have waited for ground transport that would have taken days to cross the state. Dan sat next to him, knowing he couldn't strike up a conversation but curious about this person. The flight was just under an hour and Clark barely moved a muscle. Where had it all started with him?

Dan himself had been hit by his father. Better him than Maggie; Dan had sometimes stepped in front of her so his old man couldn't get to her. It happened often enough; Maggie wasn't one to keep her mouth shut and it didn't take much to set his father off. He had gotten used to it.

Dan could still remember his heart pounding, waiting, and then just closing his eyes and letting it happen. Every once in a while his father found it particularly amusing to make Dan wait for the blow and then do nothing at all. Instead of feeling relief at that moment, Dan felt even more panic as soon as he heard his father laughing.

Maggie sometimes brought it up; it wasn't a dark secret of theirs. Dan had been bruised up and down the length of his body and Maggie had had slap marks on the backs of her legs from time to time. Those days no one asked and probably more than one kid came to school like that.

Dan hadn't ended up hating his father. Mostly he was grateful the wrath was never unleashed on his mother. Dan even managed to shed a tear when they buried him, not because of love but for the last link to the past. Of course, his love for his mother were always the primary emotion he felt. That and wanting to protect her.

Over the years he'd seen plenty of cases but never one like Petey. He could only hope it didn't mean that things were getting worse out there, which seemed to be proven true almost every day. Sometimes he called it the golden age when he talked with Deke, "Remember when it was safe to park your car on the street?" Remember when you could walk on Main Street without getting beat up. Remember when college kids' parties were harmless affairs. Remember when there were no gangs. It was a litany of complaints.

Then they would slip into a general nostalgia. Remember when you could go shopping downtown and there were theaters and several big department stores like Berger's and Hengerer's. Remember going to the movies.

Sometimes he wondered if there were too many people in the world, like the fruit fly experiment they learned about in high school. When there was a critical mass, things fell apart and the population turned mean, but overcrowding wasn't the problem in Buffalo. Maybe hopelessness pervaded with no hope for the future and that made the world a more dangerous place. Dan could only wonder at a society that turned out such citizens. But such bleak thoughts were not going to get him anywhere.

Dan returned to a hero's welcome. Police cars waited to escort Clark. Dan opted to go home first before going to the station. He turned up the heat though it should have been warm already to judge by the calendar. Then he popped into the shower to wash off the grime of the city. After he toweled off, he rummaged around the kitchen to see what he could eat. As usual there wasn't much. He considered calling Maggie but couldn't make the effort to pick up the phone. He ate a bowl of cereal standing up at the kitchen counter. Then he felt ready to contact the office and his sister.

Maggie said, "I've got the champagne chilling."

"Not so fast. I'm not sure it's over yet."

"For you it is. You brought him in. Isn't that enough?"

It should have been. Dan didn't want to explain Clark's position nor his feelings that had erupted out of nowhere. "I guess. New York was a killer. You know I'm not a big city person."

"It was just a couple of days." Frustration was evident in her voice. "Dan, you did a good job. Whatever happens from this point on is no longer your problem."

"Yeah."

"So what happened to you down there?"

"I was thinking a lot."

"About what?" She was going to pry it out of him.

"The usual."

"Miranda, you mean."

"Yup. The old broken record I can't let go of. Then I was thinking about abuse. How it starts and where the abused person ends up."

She sighed into the phone. "My dear. You have been having a hard time, haven't you?"

"I'm glad to be home even though it's a mess and there's nothing to eat."

"The magic words. I'm coming over. What do you feel like?"

"Booze."

"Besides that, obviously."

"I'll order Chinese."

"Don't worry. I'll stop on my way and pick up something. I'll surprise you."

***

Maggie appeared magically at his door in half an hour. She hugged Dan as tightly as she could. "Good to see you." He felt a bit distant. "Look what I got. Eggplant parmesan, I'll just put it in the microwave." She put a bottle of red wine on the table and unloaded a bag of groceries on the kitchen table. "This might not be what you had in mind, but we'll start with this."

"Thanks, Maggie."

She directed him as if he were one of her sons. "Open the wine and pour me a glass."

They drank in silence until the timer went off. Maggie brought out the plates. "The place looks fine to me."

"We can eat by the fireplace." Dan was beginning to revive. He stacked the wood and lit a fire.

"Heavenly."

"Who'd believe it could be this cold in May."

"Where did you grow up again?"

"I was raised by wolves in a den. You know when I was a kid I had that idea. You and I were like puppies and Mother too."

Maggie didn't ask about their father. "Not a bad image. It's true isn't it? You can feel like you're so different from your family."

"The problem is I'm not."

"Let's see. You never beat anyone as far as I know. Not even on the beat."

"I killed Miranda."

"Tell me how you reached that conclusion or have you always been letting that thought occupy your brain?"

"I didn't take care of her."

"Dan, we've been through this a thousand times. You couldn't watch her every minute. You want me to put it clearly for you. She was an alcoholic, a falling down drunk. She may have been beautiful and exciting and great in bed and whatever else, but Dan, that is not a normal way to live. You did not kill her." Maggie got it all out without taking a breath. "But why now, Dan? You were doing so well?"

"I don't know. I was in New York and I felt like she was there with me."

"Get yourself to a therapist. I'm telling you. This is way too long."

"Maybe you're right. Or maybe I was just sad. A bad case, I was away in a seedy hotel. God, I almost bought a pack of smokes."

"Remind me not to let you go to New York again."

They sat in front of the fire. "Magpie, I'm sorry."

"Don't be." She got up and refilled their glasses. "What about a movie? Unless you want to immerse yourself back into hell."

"I've done enough of that. I've been thinking I have to quit."

"You are a mess."

"I couldn't even listen to Clark's testimony. I had to leave the room. Something is wrong with me."

"Did you stop to think it might be just being human that you can't stand to hear why someone raped a little boy."

"It's my job to listen. If I can't then I'm not doing my job."

"This case has done one hell of a number on you. Why didn't you call? I would have been happy to talk to you. Instead you've been making yourself crazy with these ideas."

"I've been thinking about quitting for a while. You know that."

"Fair enough. What would you do?"

"Maybe try something political, get an office job. Teach, maybe."

"Sounds good. Look into it. How many years do you have till you can retire?"

"To do it right, way too long. I don't think I can."

"You don't want to end up a security guard."

"Could be worse."

"Not worse than that salary."

Dan smiled for the first time all evening. "I could be a detective like in the novels. Open up my own office."

"Isn't that what you want to avoid? The point is you don't want to deal with these cases anymore isn't it?"

"I wouldn't get anything like this one."

"Maybe not. But are you serious?"

"Not about being a private detective, but about leaving, yes. I still have time to get my life in order. I hope."

"So what brought up Miranda now? I thought you were feeling good lately. Even dating someone for more than two dates. What the hell happened?"

"I slapped her around. When she was drunk. God, why am I telling you this?"

"How bad? I saw her go for you more than once."

Dan was quiet. "I don't think I could even admit it to myself."

"How long did that go on?"

"One night she was passed out on the sofa. I couldn't wake her up. I gave her a slap and it felt good. God, I can't believe I'm saying this."

"She wasn't so out of it was she?"

"Maybe that's why she…"

"Dan, you can never know. She was driving drunk. The car slid in the snow."

"It couldn't have helped any. I was always angry at her."

"She was a drunk. Of course, you were angry at her."

"Maggie. I don't want this to be true confessions."

"Is there more?"

"No, thank God."

"Look, if you're not going to a counselor, tell me at least. What is they say, someone to bear witness. I'm not going to hate you, Dan."

"I was relieved when she died."

"We all were to some point."

"I was almost happy."

"Then why have you spent years with this bullshit. It's over. Miranda is gone. You treated her badly but she did the same, or worse to you. Whether it was intentional or not...."

"Mine was intentional."

"Dan, do something. Talk to someone, I'm serious about that. Or go see your priest."

"What could I say?"

"Talk about it until you make some sense of it. Then forgive yourself."

"I don't think I can."

"You don't have any choice or you'll end up in a nuthouse."

"But you see why I can't have a relationship."

"Dan, you can have a relationship with a woman who doesn't have those problems."

"Suppose I get angry at her."

"And you will. So what? You've done anger management at work. How come you can't apply that to your personal life?"

"I'm afraid. I see her lying there."

"Dan, you can feel angry without it getting out of control. You were angry at Jess and nothing happened."

"No, I broke it off."

"Was this the reason why?'

"No. I didn't trust her. I realized I didn't want the ghost world around me. Me, of all people. I have all my own ghosts. Can you imagine what that was like? Psychics, Lily Dale, the whole package. Then we didn't click right. I don't know why. I liked her but I don't think it would have gotten further."

"But she was in love with you."

"I don't know. I'm not sure."

"Okay. Let's say that's how it's going to be. You get some counseling. That's all I can say." Maggie got up from her chair and picked up the plates.

Dan had a few moments to collect himself. Maggie came back in to the room. "I've got to get going."

"Maggie, I am so sorry."

"Don't be. Like I said, I love you. That's what I'm here for." She hugged him.

After she left, Dan stayed in the chair staring at the smoldering fire for a long time. Finally, when he felt cold, he got up to go to bed. Was there any way out to get out of this?

***

That night Dan slept the sleep of the dead. When he woke, he clutched his head with a headache worse than a typical booze overdose. He was meeting Cheryl. When he got to her office, she closed the door behind him and held out her hand. "Well done. We got the match. His skin, flakes on the clothes."

"Suppose he didn't do it."

"He did enough whether he killed the boy or not. The proof is there. Irrefutable. How's that for a big word?" She smiled at him. "It could have gone either way. We could have lost him for good. You kept on it. Come on, you did a good job."

Dan took the seat she offered across from her All that time he'd considered this office his; he no longer cared. "So Cheryl, I've been doing some thinking."

She smiled, "That's always dangerous."

"And I'd like to turn in my resignation."

"No. What you need is a vacation. Take two weeks, think it over. Look, I don't know what happened but it's typical after a case, to have a letdown. It doesn't mean you throw everything away." She paused. "I was expecting you to ask for a raise."

"Would you have given it to me?"

"Sure, I can put in the paperwork. What's the next step up? See, Dan, you think about it."

"Suppose I don't want this anymore."

"I'll get you a desk job where you never have to deal with another lunatic again. How's that?"

"Only the inter office ones, you mean."

"You got that. Take the two weeks. I'm serious and I don't want to hear another word until," she looked at her calendar, "the 23rd. So you get out of here."

***

Nowhere to go. Nothing to do. Two weeks of his own thoughts scared the hell out of Dan. He could work on his apartments and get them into shape or do some work on Maggie's house. That was as far as his brain went. When he got home, he resisted the urge to crack open a beer. Instead he called Jess.

"I didn't expect to hear from you."

"I have to apologize. I know it's no excuse. I was in crisis mode and…. Jess waited for him to continue. "I wanted to let you know that I did that badly and I didn't mean to. I didn't think it would work out."

"So you're apologizing because you would have done it in a more polite way."

"If I were braver, I would have done a lot of things differently. Thank you for putting up with me and for everything else."

***

The call made him feel better; he hoped it would have a similar effect on Jess. So that was one thing off his list. Next he thought about therapy or there was Father Kazmerack. He could even try a psychic or any combination of all three to make sure he had all the bases covered.

Dan headed into the rectory office. It was after lunch so he knew Father Kazmerack would have finished serving at the kitchen they had set up for the homeless; Father Jack did his share in organizing at least a couple times a week. After Miranda died, Dan had come by often enough to remember the priest's schedule. Dan just rang the bell and went into the office.

"Dan, I thought I'd be seeing you again."

"What's everybody psychic these days?"

"Let's say, I was hoping to see you again. Congratulations."

"Can't say I'm sure he killed the boy."

"Well, you brought him in. It's up to a jury to decide that."

"It really got to me this time."

"A nasty business, even for life as we know it." Father Kazmerack motioned for Dan to sit down. "Coffee?"

"Sure."

Jack went into the kitchen and brought back two cups. "Cream, no sugar."

"What a memory you've got."

"We go way back."

"You don't need to remind me."

"Tell me, what's on your mind?"

"I don't know if I can tell you."

"You can tell a priest anything. We won't divulge a word."

"It's not that."

"We believe in forgiveness. That's what it's all about."

"So if I say a few Hail Mary's…"

"If you forgive yourself."

"So you forgive me."

"God forgives you which is the important thing."

"Just like that. Without saying a word."

"Yes. But you know you aren't alone, someone can help you."

"I talked to Maggie and I wish I hadn't."

"She's your sister."

"I shouldn't have. It's like it makes me into something else."

"Like not perfect?"

Dan sighed. "Worse than that. Like a monster."

"You're no monster. Like I said she's your sister. She knows you're not perfect. She knows all the stories."

"But I was a hero in those."

"It's the circumstances of life that can make a person a hero or not. No one is a hero 100% of the time."

Dan was struggling to begin. "You probably have things to do."

"You've got me until 3 when I go to the hospital to visit a parishioner. Take your time. Take a deep breath."

And Dan began the same version he'd told Maggie but with more detail. He told Jack about when it happened, where it happened, not sparing anything. When he finished he couldn't look the priest in the eye.

"Did you ever think of getting help for Miranda?"

"First of all, I guess I didn't think there was anything wrong with drinking. Look how I grew up. Then, I just thought if I ignored it, it would disappear. Stupid, right?"

"She never did anything about it. No AA or anything else."

"She never talked about it with me, maybe with her friends. She was tight with a couple of the teachers. They went out all the time. You know, I don't even know what Miranda did when I wasn't working, besides the drinking. It never occurred to me to ask her."

"You were together for years."

"Deke always knows what his wife is doing."

"Did Miranda know what you were doing? Your cases, what you were working on?"

"I guess not. Unless it was a big one. I didn't know what her students were doing unless one of them did something really funny. It was the same; it was work."

"That can happen when we lose touch with the important people in our lives."

"Well, I could have made more of an effort."

"Could have, should have... We all have those, Dan."

"Maybe I have more than most."

"It will be all right. I forgive you; God forgives you. Maybe now you can finally let it go. You're sorry."

"Suppose it happens again."

Father Jack suppressed a smile, "Are you going to find another beautiful and passionate Miranda out there? I don't think she exists."

"Maybe I'll do it to another woman."

"Please, try therapy. I can recommend someone." He stood up from his desk, "Dan, I'm always here for you. Don't forget that. Call me whenever you need me."

"Thank you." Dan shook his hand.

"I'll pray for you."

"If you think it'll help."

***

Dan went back to his house and surveyed it as if it were the first time he was seeing it. It badly needed a paint job and gray was not a good color; it repeated the same winter sky. He'd try a light blue this summer, something that would catch what little sun there was in the winter. Inside it was another story. He needed to replace all the furniture. He could take his time and make a home for himself. Two weeks off work, and afterwards, Dan could think everything out. He could get a safe job somewhere, maybe even teaching criminal justice if he could go back and finish his degree. Hell, if Maggie could go back to school why couldn't he?

**

Dan was in the front of the house, digging up weeds and trying to plant seeds for asters and cosmos in the flowerbeds. Deke came up behind him. "Hey, what you doing there?"

"Good question. I haven't touched the weeds out here in years." Dan got up and wiped his hands off on a towel. "How's it going?"

Deke nodded, "You're looking good. Must be all that gardening."

"It's harder than working out. Can I get you something? How about a beer?"

"Wasn't sure nature boy would still be drinking beer."

"It's Buffalo; everybody drinks beer."

"None of that sissy stuff though."

"Standard Canadian, how's that?" Dan went in the kitchen and washed his hands. He came out with two Labatts and they settled in on the porch, the weather finally warm enough to enjoy being outside.

"You're making me feel guilty. I haven't done a bit of work on my house in ages."

"Well, I got the time now."

"That's what I wanted to know, so when are you coming back?"

"Can't say that I am."

"Come on. What the fuck are you doing? Playing homemaker?"

"No, getting ready to sell it. On TV, they call it staging."

"Yeah, like we're all in theater."

"I think it works; I've been watching it on TV. So when I get this done, I'm putting it on the market."

"Where are you going to live?"

"Next to my nephew. In my house with the four units. There's an apartment that opened up; it's enough for me. I don't really need this and the big plus is I finally get rid of the ghosts. I don't know why I didn't do this years ago."

Deke shrugged. "We miss you."

Dan smiled. "I miss it too. It's strange being at home, not getting up early and going to work. The first couple of days I kind of walked around the house without a clue about what to do."

"But when are you coming back?"

"Really, Deke, I don't know. I have this leave now, six months to figure it out."

"Clark's still claiming he's innocent."

"Doesn't surprise me but let's face it, he was guilty of rape."

"Carries less than murder."

"Does anyone believe him?"

"He's got a good lawyer working on it. You know, Stevenson."

"That guy. He wins his share of cases."

"He's from New York."

"Must have seen potential for media attention." Dan surprised himself by not really caring what the outcome was. Maybe he really was making progress. "I suppose they'll be calling me to testify."

"It'll be going to court soon enough. They'll call you. That is if you can tear yourself away from your extended vacation."

Dan smiled, not rising to Deke's bait at all. "Should be able to manage. You know, I really do feel great. No worries."

"You lucky shit."

"Well, for as long as it lasts."

Dan stopped at the food co-op since he was on a health kick though it was hard to pay the higher prices for organic. He picked up a bunch of kale, and was looking at it, when Jess came up to him. "Hello, Dan."

"Jess," he smiled. "I'm trying a new tactic." He held up the kale.

"You'll hate that. I make it for Chris sometimes. It's tasteless and tough."

Dan immediately set it down. "I didn't think I'd see you in a place like this."

"My daughter wants primo junk food but it just doesn't taste that good. How are you doing?"

"Trying to sort out some stuff. I'm taking time off work."

"Well, good luck."

"It's been nice seeing you." And it was. Dan watched her as she made her way down the aisle. She had her hair up in a ponytail which made her look much younger than usual. He wanted to catch up with her and ask if she wanted to have a coffee but he focused on the broccoli instead. It was a vegetable he had always hated. Carrots were safe and lettuce was always good. He put a head of romaine in his cart. By the time he made his way through the store, he usually ended up picking up prepared food to eat. Jess was there looking at the sushi. "It's everywhere now. Did you ever notice that?"

"Do you like it?"

"Not particularly. Do you?"

"I like the wasabi, but with my stomach..."

Jess smiled at him. "I remember."

"Are you in a hurry? Would you like to have a coffee?"

She eyed the food bar. "We can get it here and sit outside. It always seems like such a luxury to eat outside finally. What a cold spring."

"It still could be."

"Still the optimist."

They found a corner table in the sunlight. 'Jess, I have to apologize."

"You already have."

"I guess I want to know if you can forgive me."

"I can. I didn't want to but.." She smiled. "So what are you going to do now that you're not working?"

"I've got the house on the market. I'm done with that. I'm living over on Richmond now. I've got a one bedroom and it's okay. I'm getting rid of my old junk, little by little; deciding what to save and what to toss. Some of it, I'm just sticking in storage. What about you? How is Chris doing?"

"That's the good news. She's with me for the summer."

"All right. How did you manage that?"

"Threats to my ex. She's coming in two weeks."

"I'm happy for you."

"We're going to San Francisco for a week."

"Wow."

"I do have to compete with her dad."

"I'm glad we can sit like this and talk."

"I don't hate you, Dan."

"Even if I deserve it."

"Even if." She downed the rest of her coffee with soy milk. "Soy grows on you."

"Yes, I like it. Probably most of what we eat is loaded with it anyway. Might as well eat it directly."

"You look like you're in good spirits."

"It's taken me a long time."

"Are you going back to work?"

"I haven't decided. This break has been the best thing I could have done. I'm seeing a therapist."

"Good. You must be making progress."

"I think so. Maybe I'm getting rid of all the past."

"Miranda, you mean."

"Mostly guilt."

"That's a lot to take on."

"Yeah."

"So Dan, I'm glad you're doing well."

"I'm glad to see you and very glad things got straightened out with Chris." Dan got up and gave her a hug. "You didn't get your shopping done. I can help you navigate through all the health food, even make some recommendations."

"No, thanks. I can manage."

***

The realization that Dan never understood Miranda was still plaguing him. Dan found the number in his old agenda. He had no idea if Liz still lived in that big house where the party was held the night Miranda died. He took a deep breath as he picked up the phone. He chose a café, a neutral spot at 4 in the afternoon, an hour when a teacher could be free.

He held out his hand to her and then went to the counter and got her a coffee. "Thanks for coming."

"Maybe I've been waiting a long time for you to call."

Dan was surprised, "Really?"

"We acted like it never happened, that either Miranda was still here or she never existed."

"You're right. I couldn't accept it. I've been trying to figure all that out." Dan looked at her face, "I have the feeling I missed something. I didn't really know what she wanted. Maybe I didn't have much of an idea of what she was all about."

"Well, you know how much she wanted a baby."

"Sure. That much I knew; everybody did. But with the drinking…"

"She wasn't worried; she said that she'd love the child no matter what." Dan swallowed hard. "She knew you didn't want the baby."

"It wasn't that I didn't want one. I was worried what could happen, the alcohol. You talked about that with her. She never told me."

"Look, I know the drinking was what she was for you. But I had something else. I loved Miranda, we talked every day, about everything." Liz's voice broke. "She had a beautiful spirit; she was a good old soul."

"Generous."

"You'll never know the half of it, especially with the kids, at work."

"With me."

"Yes. She forgave you, so you don't have to worry about that."

"What did she really want?"

"I don't know. What everyone wants I suppose, she wanted to be happy; she wanted a life like she never had when she was growing up. She wanted a house full of children. She wanted to paint. Remember that big red abstract painting. I have it hanging in my living room. She left it to me."

Dan could barely remember it but Miranda had left a detailed will which made him realize how long she must have been thinking about death. Dan could almost smell the oil paints and turpentine; she'd stopped when she got pregnant worrying about the toxicity of the paints and then she never went back to it. He didn't have a single painting. "I remember that smell of paint."

"She was good."

"I couldn't tell."

"That's too bad."

"She didn't leave me any."

"There weren't that many, just a few. Maggie's got one."

Dan flashed on it, still hanging in her bedroom. "Miranda thought I couldn't appreciate her painting."

"She thought you had enough with the house and everything else in it."

"Did you talk to her about dying?"

"Miranda thought she'd die young. An astrologer told her that when she was sixteen and she never forgot it."

"That person should be shot."

Liz shrugged, "It wasn't like she took it as gospel; it was more like a feeling, or maybe it's just what she wanted all along." She waited a couple of minutes and then took out some photos. "I figured you might want to see these. God, my kids missed her. For years." She passed each photo to Dan and he looked at them slowly. There were pictures of Liz and her children from the time they were born. Miranda was the godmother to the oldest and was in every photo. "Steve thought she was an angel."

"I had no idea."

"She was part of us."

"Where was I all that time?"

"Working. That's what Miranda always said."

"I was."

"Sure."

"Was there anything else I should know?" Dan felt like he was asking an expert on Miranda.

"She worried about getting old."

"Really? She was so beautiful."

"Well, getting pregnant before it was too late; the forties were coming and then, she was always the pretty one who got all the attention. Getting older is hard when you set such store by it."

"She never was that vain."

"No, but she always got special treatment. No matter where we went Miranda got an extra drink or a free dessert. Then I think she worried you'd leave her."

Dan had to smile. "She's dead and I can't leave her even now. I never gave her any reason to think that."

"Sometimes, it's just insecurity."

"She gave me more reason." Dan got defensive.

"She was never in love with them. It was part of that chaos. You knew that didn't you?"

"Yes. It didn't help though."

"I'm sure it didn't. Do you think you'll be able to work this out?"

"God, I don't know. It's been messing with my mind for years now. Every time I think I finally can put it to rest, something else comes up. For years I couldn't admit to myself that I hit her."

Liz nodded. "She told me."

"It was like hitting an innocent creature. I am well aware of that. What did she say?"

"She thought she deserved it."

"Oh, my God, no." Dan put his head in his hands.

"I told her no one deserves that. She was going to see a therapist after she lost the baby but she couldn't do it. She was lost."

"It was my fault."

"It's not all about you. Miranda was like an open wound. The last weeks she was worse. She had vodka with her in her car; she gave me a ride home one day and I saw it. I suppose she drank during the day but I honestly can't say. She held it pretty well at work. I don't know if anyone else there knew. You bore the brunt of it."

Dan remembered the screaming, the arguments. The nights when he got home and she was passed out were a relief. The body that he carried like a dead weight and placed on the bed came back to him; he could almost feel it in his arms. "It's no excuse, I know, but it was hard."

"No kidding. I saw that too. Fury, I guess you could call it. You never knew what would trigger her."

"God, I am so so sorry."

"Dan, I know that. Everyone knows that. Miranda is gone and has been for years. Let her rest."

"That's what I'm trying to do." Dan prepared himself to ask the last question. "So, do you really think she wanted to die?"

"There was never any evidence for that. We'll never know. She was drunk; it could have been a moment blanking out at the wheel. She was having fun at work those last weeks. Her students were putting on a play and she was into it. She had the costumes ready so I really don't know."

"I guess we never will."

"Let it go, Dan. It's enough already."

"Believe me, I'm trying. I've got the house on the market."

"Let me come over and see it one last time."

"Sure. I have to get rid of stuff. I still have some boxes; if there's anything you want."

"Thank you, but I don't think I could bear it."

"I understand."

"Well, I've got to go and pick up Kimberly at her dance class."

Dan smiled. "Your girls must be grown up by now."

"Almost there. It goes by so fast."

"Liz, thank you. I mean it."

"Sure."

Chapter Fourteen

Since he had moved out of the house, Dan was sleeping better. That and the fact he wasn't seeing the aftermath of violence on people's lives gave him some breathing room. It was a relief not to have to see a dead body or a battered one. He was distancing himself from the violence of the world around him. He stopped watching the news altogether and instead watched movies, classics he compiled from a list and ordered online alphabetically online. He was now on the B's having just seen"A Bride for Henry." These were light films that made him smile. Soon enough he'd start on the dramas.

Just how long he could inhabit this bubble world wasn't clear. He calculated his finances and came to the conclusion he had a margin of three more months before he had to act.

***

Dan knotted his tie and looked at himself in the mirror. He was in his new black suit with just a small pattern; nothing suggesting mafia, just a subtle line. He wore a new blue shirt, TV blue he called it since he read in the paper that it was the most flattering color to wear on television. Not that he was going to be on TV; but he made an effort. He finally had gotten around to replenishing his wardrobe and even got a more stylish haircut. "I look like a politician." He smiled at his reflection. "Not too bad for my age anyway."

It was the big day, the day Dan was testifying in the Clark trial. He followed none of it in the news and just planned to leave the courtroom directly after the testimony. He got there to find it crowded with journalists filling up the seats in the back. Dan sat down and observed the courtroom. He felt nostalgic; he couldn't count the number of times he'd testified. Of course, most weren't for such high profile cases.

***

Linda Jackson looked like she had given up on life, her hair was a frizzy mess and her face was gaunt. Her husband, not looking much better, sat next to her. Aaron Clark didn't look bad, considering Dan last saw him in the hospital. He was dressed in a dark suit with freshly cut hair and almost a healthy glow about him. The last thing Clark looked like was a child murderer. Rather, he looked like a fairly successful businessman which was the image the defense was aiming for. Dan wondered if the defense had something lined up, some surprise they were going to pull out of the bag at the last minute like on the old Perry Mason shows.

Dan settled in and tried to focus on the proceedings without getting emotionally caught up in the case. The prosecution was going over the details. He and Deke would be called though Deke hadn't shown up yet. A high profile case yet nobody else from the office was there. Cheryl could be avoiding more publicity or more likely just couldn't be spared. He'd been away from the office so he had no idea as to what was happening.

Dan was caught off guard when his name was called. He answered the best he could trying not to see the body, the snow, that day in the winter. He could almost feel his wet feet sliding down the small ravine to the creek. He had to focus his mind on the questions and not be distracted. He had to be really badly off if he couldn't keep his mind on the questions. The forensic report was there and after such a long time, it still shocked. Dan fought off the emotion and just made it to the end of the defense trying to throw some doubt onto the situation. Considering the crime and the evidence, that was not an easy task. Dan glanced over at the jury who showed none of the slack jawed fatigue that most jurors showed while they were thinking about what to have for lunch or what their families were doing without them. No, this jury was on high alert.

Dan left the courtroom immediately and headed for his car. Once he got inside, he closed the door, turned on the engine and put his aching head in his hands.

There was no one left that he could bother. He didn't want to call Father Jack or Maggie since he was still embarrassed by what he'd told his sister. When he got to his new home which he wasn't quite sure he could even give call home, Dan just threw together a few things in a bag.

The drive down to Erie, Pennsylvania following the lake was faster and prettier than he'd expected. When he got to the center of the city, he asked for directions to the cemetery at a donut shop. Erie Cemetery was big and reminiscent of Forest Lawn in Buffalo. Dan went to the office at the gate to see if he could get a map or some information. The man in the reception area frowned, "Let's see if I can look it up. We try to keep up to date. Even got walkers."

"Walkers?"

"People who walk the graves and write down the names. Otherwise, we wouldn't have a clue who's here anymore. Lots of these are abandoned. The cemetery dates from 1850, so figure. The family dies and then there just isn't anybody to come anymore."

Dan spelled the name for him and waited. "Section E 18, you can go towards the left and follow the arrows."

"Can I get some flowers around here?"

"Sure. There's a florist right outside the cemetery if you drive back out and hang a right."

"Thanks." For a moment, Dan contemplated keeping on, driving past the florist right back on the highway to Buffalo but something made him stop. He picked out a bunch of gladiolas, a flower he thought was masculine, and somewhat funereal having seen them at every funeral he'd ever attended. He chose red, an imposing bright color for a man he barely remembered.

Following instructions, Dan drove to a part of the cemetery that was filled with small gravestones. There were no elaborate monuments or statues but a smattering of American flags for the veterans. After walking through several rows, he finally spotted the one he was looking for: his grandparents: Daniel Kiraly, Elisa Kiraly. He was the third Daniel and the last.

"The end of the line. It won't happen anymore." Dan said it as he bent down to put the flowers in a small urn that was there. He wondered who had put it there and when the last time was that it had been used; maybe it had been his mother. She'd taken on those responsibilities. Dan went to find a faucet thinking that the purpose of the flowers was to give you busy work, something to fuss about.

Once his grandfather had died, his trips to Erie stopped with the boat trips on the lake a memory of sunlight shimmering on the water. His father hated boats; the closest he got to the water was fishing on the break wall off the river.

His father was utterly silent when his grandfather was anywhere near. When Dan was young, he liked the visits to Erie for that reason; his father was transformed into a different being, a quiet respectful person who never yelled at anyone.

His grandfather had come with the Russians to work in shipbuilding. Dan always had a romantic notion of ships and had once dreamt of sailing around the world. That lasted until a boat trip on the lake left him so seasick he begged his buddies from work on the boat to let him off and of course, they never let him forget it.

He never knew Elisa, his grandmother; it was a family secret that she took off and left her husband while everyone pretended she had died. Dan didn't find out the truth until his grandfather died. Now, he wondered if she had been escaping what his own mother had to live with. But she had been buried here, so at some point she had returned; maybe the family brought her back after her death.

There was no trace of his grandmother in his stack of pictures and papers; she'd been excised from their lives. There might be a chance Maggie would know; she had a good memory and felt responsible for keeping family records for the boys. She had photo albums she'd put together. Dan had resisted the urge to hand over his boxes of pictures to her; it wasn't her burden to go through them.

Dan did remember the funeral in bits and flashes since it was the first he'd ever attended. Dan and Maggie had been taken out of school for the event and they had to sit silently the length of the trip to Erie. His mother had objected, but his father insisted on them coming. "They're old enough. What you gonna do, protect them for the rest of their lives? People die." He shrugged.

His mother tried to steer him away from the open casket, but Dan was fascinated by the waxen figure with a contorted face that looked nothing like his muscular grandfather. The image had stayed with him when he closed his eyes. He tried shutting them tightly so that all he could see was black but the white shirt peeked through followed by the plastic looking face.

The Catholic Church was packed; his grandfather was respected at work and had a big circle of friends who crowded his house afterwards. Dan sat on the staircase with Maggie, the only two children in attendance. People crowded past them to go up the stairs to the bathroom. One elderly woman stopped to pat his head. Years later, his own father's funeral had been a small affair in contrast and his mother's had been downright tragic with drinks flowing. So in retrospect, Dan realized his first funeral hadn't been so terrible.

He peered at the faded lettering on the stone. He would ask to be cremated so there would be no need for this. His ashes scattered on the lake would be a solution, but it really didn't matter since he'd no longer be here. He supposed it would be Maggie who'd take care of things unless something terrible happened to her. Now that would be something to pray for, keep Maggie safe from harm.

He felt free as he walked to his car. Dan was in no hurry to get back home so he drove to the beach. Erie was smaller than Buffalo. The light off the lake was bright and clear. He imagined he could see all the way across to Canada. The God-damned lake; he wondered why he had ever left. He had those dreams years ago of traveling to Europe and China and only made it across the border to Canada.

"There's time. I could start with Hungary. What was it that was coursing through his veins? Retrace all the steps to find the answers and see the country of his family of origin.

When he got back to the apartment he saw it for what it was. A dump. He'd been renting these places out for so many years. The space was cramped and there was a grime that penetrated all the surfaces, evidence that the people who had lived there never cared, nor did he. He'd just spent weeks cleaning out his house so he didn't feel up to the task of taking on another place. Even his faithful cleaning woman could only do so much.

Dan surveyed the walls, a paint job was in order. Then he'd work on the wood. Todd never complained, but then maybe he didn't notice. Middle age was when it hit and he actually began to notice where he was living. Now Dan was aiming for a sense of home.

His phone snapped him out of his reverie. Deke said, "I thought you'd want to know. He's declared guilty. Took less than an hour for the jury to decide."

"Thanks for calling." Dan pondered the decision. Yes, it was good news. It was over, finally.

About Terez Peipins

Terez Peipins is a writer of Latvian descent from Western New York. Her poetry, fiction, and essays have appeared in publications both in the United States and abroad. She is the author of four chapbooks of poetry and three novels, *The Shadow of Silver Birch, Three Bonds Unbroken,* and *Snow Clues, and River Clues. River Clues* is the second book in the Dan Kiraly detective series. She divides her time between Buffalo, New York, and Barcelona, Spain.

"A moving character-driven story of a decent cope investigating the brutal murder of a child while trying, at the same time, to put his life back together."
-David C. Hall, author of Barcelona Skyline

"Peipins offer a fascinating and thrilling novel!" Jose Luis Munoz

Social Media

Facebook: https://www.facebook.com/terez.peipins
Facebook: https://www.facebook.com/TeresaPeipins
I use this page for prompts for other writers, poetry, and fiction.
 Goodreads:
https://www.goodreads.com/author/show/14343599.Terez_%20Peipins
LinkedIn: https://www.linkedin.com/in/teresa-peipins19ab1a26/?original_referer=
Twitter: https://twitter.com/TerezP @TerezP
Blog: http://peipins.blogspot.com/
Instagram:
https://www.instagram.com/terezpeipins/%20@TerezP%20

https://m.facebook.com/Snow-Clues-A-Dan-Kiraly-Mystery-891160934357118/?paipv=1

Acknowledgements

I would like to thank Lucy Peipins and Barry Flanagan for their help in reviewing and editing the manuscript.
I am grateful to Jose Luis Munoz has taken time from his busy writing schedule to read my crime novel in English.

Other books by Terez Peipins

River Clues A Dan Kiraly Mystery

In the matter of just a few days the bodies of two women float up in the Niagara River. Are the two deaths connected? Detective Dan Kiraly must find out with the help of his two partners, Clarisse and Deke. Meanwhile Kiraly's personal life heats up at the same time as he faces the dilemmas of a changing world.

https://www.amazon.com/dp/B09PLKZZCN

Made in the USA
Middletown, DE
21 February 2023

24991930R00110